"Lindy, Come Back Home With Me Right Now," Thad Insisted.

"Unless you're going to arrest me, I'll assume I'm free to go," Lindy said.

Thad squared his shoulders. "Lindy, I didn't want to resort to this, but you're a chicken. A coward. A lily-livered wimp. All talk and no action."

Lindy could almost feel the steam coming out of her ears. "How dare you!"

"Go ahead, slap me. Isn't that what you want to do?"

She'd sworn she wouldn't slap him, but she'd never said anything about kicking. She struck him swiftly with the heel of her cowboy boot. She regretted it right away.

"Oh, Thad," Lindy said. "I'm sorry!"

"Not half as sorry as I am," he said wryly. A smile spread slowly across his face. "Guess what, Lindy? You just assaulted an officer. You are under arrest!"

Dear Reader,

When I think of autumn, I think of cool, crisp November nights curled up by the fire . . . reading a red-hot Silhouette Desire novel. Now, I know not all of you live in cooler climes, but I'm sure you, too, can conjure up visions of long, cozy nights with the hero of your dreams.

Speaking of heroes, Dixie Browning has created a wonderful one in MacCasky Ford, the hero of her *Man of the Month* book, *Not a Marrying Man*. Mac is a man you'll never forget, and he certainly meets his match in Banner Keaton.

November is also a time of homecoming, and Leslie Davis Guccione has been "away from home" for far too long. I know everyone will be glad to see her back with *A Gallant Gentleman*. And if you're looking for something tender, provocative and inspirational, don't miss Ashley Summer's *Heart's Ease*. This story is one I feel very strongly about, and I'd be interested in hearing how you like it.

Rounding out November are a delicious love story from Raye Morgan, *Baby Aboard,* a fiery romp by Carole Buck, *Red-Hot Satin,* and a sexy, spritely tale by Karen Leabo, *Lindy and the Law.*

So, until next month, happy reading!

Lucia Macro
Senior Editor

KAREN
LEABO

LINDY AND THE LAW

SILHOUETTE *Desire*®

Published by Silhouette Books New York

America's Publisher of Contemporary Romance

SILHOUETTE BOOKS
300 East 42nd St., New York, N.Y. 10017

LINDY AND THE LAW

ISBN: 0-373-05676-1

First Silhouette Books printing November 1991

Printed in the U.S.A.

Books by Karen Leabo

Silhouette Desire

Close Quarters #629
Lindy and the Law #676

Silhouette Romance

Roses Have Thorns #648
Ten Days in Paradise #692
Domestic Bliss #707
Full Bloom #731
Smart Stuff #764
Runaway Bride #797

KAREN LEABO

credits her fourth-grade teacher with initially sparking her interest in creative writing. She was determined at an early age to have her work published. When she was in the eighth grade, she wrote a children's book and convinced her school-yearbook publisher to put it in print.

Karen was born and raised in Dallas but now lives in Kansas City, Missouri. She has worked as a magazine art director, a free-lance writer and a textbook editor. Now she keeps herself busy full-time writing about romance.

One

——

Only fifteen more miles to Corrigan. She would make it in plenty of time. Still, prompted by guilt at her own tardiness, Lindy Shapiro nudged the gas pedal of her '63 Cadillac convertible another centimeter closer to the floor.

As she approached the town of Winstonia she glanced into the rearview mirror, a reflex action. Not another car was in sight, behind or ahead of her. The afternoon was hot and still, the East Texas highway smooth and straight. She had new tires, new brakes, and steering so responsive she could have guided the car through an obstacle course with her little finger. She let the speedometer needle inch toward seventy as the wind whipped through her hair.

By the time she saw the beige patrol car squatting behind a clump of mesquite it was too late. She resisted slamming on the brakes and instead downshifted and pulled her foot off the gas, but the effort gained her nothing. Red and blue lights flashed angrily at her in the mirror.

Lindy didn't waste any time cursing her luck, or the ill timing of the highway patrolman who pulled up behind her. She eased the huge car onto the dusty shoulder, her mind already teeming with possible excuses for her lead foot. The truth was pretty good. A creative embellishment might work even better.

"Afternoon, officer," she called out to the patrolman who climbed out of the beige car. She appraised him quickly, inhaling sharply as she did. He was six-foot or more, without an ounce of fat on his well-muscled body—and looked tough. He'd be the no-nonsense type who worked out at the YMCA and took his job seriously. He posed a definite challenge.

As he approached at a maddeningly slow saunter, she flashed what she hoped was a captivating smile and pushed her sunglasses on top of her head. "Is there a problem?"

To Lindy's discouragement, the man didn't smile back. His mouth was set in a grim, straight line that could have been chiseled in stone. *Halsey,* his name tag read. Halsey, Halsey. The name didn't ring any bells, but she'd been away from the area for quite a while.

"Let me see your license, please," he said in a Clint Eastwood deadpan.

She was already digging through her braided-rope handbag. "I wasn't speeding, was I?" she said with all the youthful innocence she could muster. Unfortunately the officer didn't appear to be susceptible to it.

He took her license and silently studied it. His expression never changed, and Lindy couldn't even read his eyes, shadowed as they were by the brim of his hat. She thought perhaps they were blue, but she wasn't sure.

"I guess I wouldn't be surprised if I was accidently speeding," she said to fill the tense silence. "I'm on my way to my sister's wedding in Corrigan. I had car trouble this morning just outside of Wichita Falls, and I'm afraid it put me behind schedule. I know, I know, I shouldn't exceed the speed limit. I mean, it's not a matter of life and death, but it is awfully important to my family that I make it on time—"

"Your license is expired," he said.

"What?"

"Last month. And your car tags lapsed in March. Is this your car?"

"Of course it is!" she snapped, bristling. Then, remembering herself, she smiled again. "Like it?" No man, not even a stone-faced cop, could resist a classic candy-apple red Cadillac convertible with a V-8 under the hood.

He didn't answer her. "Any particular reason a Washington resident is driving a car with California plates? In Texas?"

"I've moved around a lot," she explained with a nervous laugh. "Sometimes it's hard to keep all that stuff current. Anyway, I'm moving back to Texas, now, as you can see." She nodded toward the pile of boxes in the back seat. "I'll see to the driver's license and plates first thing Monday morning."

"Were you aware, Miss Shapiro, that you were driving seventy-one in a fifty-five?"

"Gosh, no, I thought the limit was sixty-five," she said, aiming for a bewildered tone. At least it was the truth. She wouldn't have deliberately pushed her luck quite as far as she had. *Seventy-one in a fifty-five.* At ten dollars for each mile over...

He surveyed her calmly, as if gauging the sincerity of her words. She stared up at him with placating eyes, and wondered if she might be able to squeeze out a few tears. Her sister Claire would kill her—torture her first and then kill her—if she ruined this wedding by not showing up. It was bad enough she'd missed the rehearsal, and she'd promised Claire faithfully that she would get to the church in plenty of time for the actual event. Now this overconscientious lawman was ruining everything.

Waiting for his verdict made her edgy. "Are you going to write me a ticket or not?" she asked, dropping any overt attempt at charm, since it wasn't working, anyway. "If so, could you get on with it? I really do have a wedding to get to."

His rigid face softened ever so slightly, and Lindy thought for sure she was going to get a break, until he tipped the brim of his hat and she got a good glimpse of his eyes. They were brown—an intense, disturbing, velvety brown that made her mouth grow dry—and they held a look of complete inflexibility.

"You'll have to come with me, Miss Shapiro," he said at last.

"What?"

"I said, you'll have to—"

"I heard what you said. You don't actually mean to arrest me, do you?"

"I should."

She bit off the angry retort that threatened to erupt and tried to think what strategy she should employ next. This was no longer a simple inconvenience. She had a total of eighteen dollars and a gasoline credit card on her—not enough to bail herself out of jail. Somehow, some way, she had to convince this man to let her go.

She didn't like to do it, but she'd have to play her ace in the hole. She took a pen and an old envelope out of her purse. "What's your first name, Officer Halsey?"

"That's *Sheriff* Halsey. Thad Halsey." He pointed to the badge pinned to his khaki shirt. "Do you need further identification?"

She scribbled down his name. Just her luck—she'd been caught by the county sheriff himself! "That won't be necessary. I'm sure my mother knows exactly who you are," she said casually. "My mother—Marianne Shapiro?"

At last, at long last, she got a reaction out of him, though not exactly the one she'd hoped for. "Judge Shapiro is your mother? How about that. Just last week she was saying she wanted to crack down on speeders."

So much for family connections. Lindy chewed on her bottom lip and waited for inspiration, but none came.

Sheriff Thad Halsey was once again curt and emotionless. "I wasn't planning to arrest you," he said as he printed carefully into his citation book, "but I will give you a ticket. And I can't let you drive with an expired license and expired plates. You'll have to come with me to the sheriff's office and make arrangements for some other transportation."

"Oh, no, really, you can't..." But obviously he could. "I can't just leave my car here on the side of the road," she said. "What about all my things?"

"Put the top up and lock it," he suggested. "I'll send someone to pick it up."

"It's only fifteen more miles," she entreated. "I'll drive like my grandmother."

He shook his head.

She sighed again and switched on the ignition so she could run the top and the windows up. Then the odious man escorted her to his sturdy Oldsmobile with its Scanlon County Sheriff's Department emblem on the door. At least he didn't balk when she insisted on bringing an armload of stuff with her.

She sat in the back seat, clutching her purse as well as a silver-wrapped package and a black plastic garment bag. If by some miracle she did make it to Claire's wedding, she refused to show up without a gift or her bridesmaid's dress.

The air conditioner was on full blast as the car got under way, but little of the cool air reached the back seat and Lindy became uncomfortably aware of her rumpled condition. She'd been on the road for seven days, mostly with the top down.

She leaned up so she could see herself in the rearview mirror. Even though her image was obscured by the wire

mesh that separated back seat from front, she was aghast at
the vision that greeted her. Her shaggy blond hair looked as
if it hadn't seen a comb for days, and her face was sun-
burned. She definitely was not bridesmaid material.

With a grimace she slumped back into her seat and shifted
her gaze to the back of her antagonizer's head. As if aware
of her scrutiny, he flipped off his hat and finger-combed his
thick, caramel-colored hair. His hands and forearms were
strong-looking and tanned, as was his face and the back of
his neck. She wondered how much of the rest of him sported
that warm, golden-brown color.

Gawd, Lindy, she thought, is nothing sacred to you? The
man represented law and order, not to mention the fact that
he was putting her in a terrible bind, and she was entertaining sexy thoughts about what he might look like under that
starched uniform.

"Something funny?" he asked, gazing at her in the rearview mirror.

She puckered her mouth to obliterate the look of amusement that had sneaked up on her. "Not really. I was just
wondering what it would take to make you crack a smile,"
she improvised. "Don't you find anything amusing?"

"Not at the moment. In fact, women who try to get by on
sheer cuteness don't amuse me at all."

"I wasn't asking if you found *me* amusing," she said,
trying not to take offense. He'd done nothing more than
observe the truth. There was more to her than looks, of
course, but curly blond hair, an upturned nose and long legs
had gotten her out of more than one sticky situation. Unfortunately today her physical charms were striking out.
"I'm talking about how you address life in general," she
persisted. "I mean, I'm the one who's going to ruin her little sister's wedding by not showing up, and possibly alien-
ate my entire extended family, but *my* face doesn't look like
a brick wall."

"No, I don't suppose it does," he agreed before returning his attention to the road.

She sighed. There was no use talking to the cretin, even if he did have a torso worthy of a Greek sculptor's attention. If there was one thing she couldn't abide it was someone who didn't talk.

Winstonia was larger than her hometown of Corrigan, with two banks, a car dealership and its own shopping mall, but still it was pretty dinky for the county seat, Lindy had always thought. Then again, Scanlon was one of the smallest counties in Texas. Thad pulled up in front of the ancient courthouse, which housed the sheriff's office and county jail.

Lindy hadn't been inside the old courthouse in years. She hoped it had air-conditioning and a water fountain. She'd drunk the last root beer from her cooler two hundred miles back.

An elderly woman with a round, red face smiled from behind the reception desk as they entered the sheriff's office. "Howdy, Thad," she said, then cast a questioning look toward Lindy.

"Hey, Belva. The lady needs to make a call." He nodded toward a pay phone on the wall of the waiting area, then watched for a moment as Lindy fished in her purse for a quarter.

Belva demanded his attention with a handful of pink message slips. He glanced through them, but his eyes were drawn inexorably to the leggy blonde standing by the pay phone. A pair of full-cut navy shorts and a baggy T-shirt bearing a beer logo did little to disguise a taut, athletic body.

In some ways he wished he hadn't treated her so coldly. It hadn't been easy. He'd felt himself responding to her winsome smile and her dancing green eyes, but if he'd softened toward her, even a tiny bit, he might have been tempted to let her off the hook. So it was just as well he'd behaved like a humorless stick-in-the-mud. A woman like her could play havoc with his sense of duty.

"Who is she?" Belva whispered.

"Judge Shapiro's daughter," he said under his breath.

"You mean that crazy Lindy? She hasn't been around here in years." But the older woman was smiling fondly. "I remember her as a little girl. She really shined, that one did." The smile faded. "She took it hard when her father died, you know. Marianne indulged her, I'm afraid—let her run wild all over the county."

"She's broadened her territory considerably," Thad said dryly. "And wait till you see what she's driving—oh, that reminds me." He used Belva's dispatch radio to locate two of his deputies and directed them to collect Lindy's car.

Just as he finished his call, an indelicate curse reverberated through the room. He looked up sharply to see Lindy Shapiro seething at the phone.

"Problem?" he asked.

"No one's home. They must all be at the church already, but I can't seem to raise anyone there, either." Then she glared up at him. "My sister will strangle me with her bare hands for ruining her wedding. With my dying breath, do you know who I'm going to blame?"

He felt the corner of his mouth twitch, but he kept it in check. "How about yourself, for driving around with an expired license and tags? For that matter, you could have allowed more traveling time—"

"I allowed myself a whole week to get here from Seattle. I just ran into more delays than I counted on—flat tires, a cracked radiator hose, not to mention getting lost in Colorado for half a day. Who'd have thought I'd get this far, only to be stopped a mere fifteen miles from the church?" She sank into one of the plastic chairs lining the wall, clutching the garment bag to her and looking so dejected that only a heartless barbarian could have remained unmoved.

Thad exchanged a look with Belva.

"It's a pretty slow day," the gray-headed woman observed casually.

Damn. He was going to do it. "I have to drive into Corrigan," he said to Lindy. "I suppose I could take you along and drop you off someplace—"

Lindy popped out of her chair as if she'd been spring-loaded and beamed at him like a lighthouse. "Oh, thank you, Sheriff Halsey. You may have just saved my family the inconvenience of disowning me. Could you...would you mind if I took just a moment to freshen up?"

He shrugged and pointed to the ladies' room. She scooted into it, emerging less than five minutes later looking freshly scrubbed. She smelled pretty good, too, he noticed after she'd gathered up her things and waltzed past him out the door. Certainly not like that green soap in the bathroom.

"You can ride in the front seat," he said as he unlocked the passenger door. He'd concluded she wasn't armed or dangerous. Well, not armed, anyway.

"I'd prefer to sit in the back, actually," she said. "I was planning on changing clothes while you drive."

Thad froze only for a moment before turning and opening the back, as she'd requested.

"It's all right, isn't it? I mean, your windows are tinted. And surely I can count on an upstanding lawman like yourself not to peek."

After six years working for the Dallas PD, nothing much could shock Thad. Still, the idea of Judge Shapiro's live-wire daughter disrobing in his back seat had an unsettling effect. She was just waiting for him to object, however, so he didn't.

He tried, very hard, to keep his eyes glued steadfastly to the road ahead of them as he drove toward Corrigan. But after several minutes of listening to the soft sounds of fabric brushing fabric, and the rustle of plastic and the whisper of something he imagined to be chiffon, he found his gaze sliding to the rearview mirror.

He saw only a flash of golden skin—an arm? A leg? His glance had been too quick for him to be sure.

"I'm finished changing," she said after another couple of minutes. "All I have to do now is put on a little makeup and comb my hair. How much farther?"

"Six miles."

"No problem," she said breezily.

He chanced another look in the mirror. She now wore a pale peach dress with puffy sleeves and bows on the shoulders, and was busy applying a shimmering peach substance to her eyelids.

She looked up and caught his eye. "Instant bridesmaid. What do you think?"

He thought she was entirely too cute for her own good, but he refrained from pointing that out. He'd heard quite a lot about Lindy Shapiro in the four years he'd lived in Scanlon County. Mostly people said she was charming but flaky, and not at all like her sensible mother. Perhaps if Lindy weren't so damned perky she might be forced to make her way in the world on something besides chutzpah.

Still, she hadn't pulled anything over on him. He was proud of that fact. The only reason he was giving her a ride to her sister's wedding was for Judge Shapiro. She'd no doubt forked out a bundle to marry off her youngest, and she wouldn't want to see the affair ruined by her other, more inconsiderate daughter. Lindy's legs had nothing to do with his good deed.

"Do you know where St. Andrew's is?" she asked a few minutes later. Corrigan was hardly more than a wide place in the road, but Lindy felt a pleasant shimmering of nostalgia as they approached the city limits of her hometown.

"On Third Street, right?"

"Right. Just pull up in front and I'll dash inside." Despite the urgency of her sister's wedding, Lindy felt suddenly saddened at the prospect of ending her adventure with the sheriff. He was inflexible, utterly humorless, and as talkative as a tree stump, true, but she sensed his dearth of words wasn't due to a similar sparseness of brainwaves. She might have enjoyed drawing him out, especially since she suspected he wasn't nearly as bored and irritated by her as he would have her believe.

"Ah, well," she murmured under her breath.

The first person she saw when they pulled up to the church was her brother Kevin, standing on the front steps in his tux and looking harried. The late-afternoon sunlight gleamed off hair even blonder than hers.

"Thanks for the ride," she said as she tried to open her door. "Oops, I forgot. No door handles back here."

"I'll have to open it from the outside." He left the motor running as he came around the car, seemingly not in any hurry. Just as he put the key in the door Kevin smiled and waved. Halsey paused to call out a greeting, and the two men were soon engaged in an animated exchange that Lindy couldn't hear. The conscientious sheriff had apparently forgotten about her.

She rapped on the window and scowled. He managed to tear himself away long enough to unlock the door.

Kevin's jaw dropped when he saw his sister emerging from the sheriff's car. "What in the hell kinda trouble did you get into, sis?" he asked, even as he enveloped her in a hug. "We've been worried sick about you."

"It's a long story," she answered. "But at least I'm here."

"Yeah, thanks, Thad, for getting her here," Kevin said. "You coming to the wedding?"

"I'd like to, but I'm on duty for another hour."

"You're coming to the reception, though," he said, as if it were a foregone conclusion. "With Pete and the Pit Bulls playing, it should be a hoot. You can tell me the real story of how you hooked up with my sister. I can guaran-damn-tee ya we won't get the straight scoop from her."

"Kevin!" Lindy objected as she handed him some of her things to carry. "You make it sound like I'm some kind of pathological liar."

"A good storyteller," he corrected her. He looked at his watch. "Jeez Louise, it's almost time. We better get inside. Thanks again, Thad."

"Yeah, thanks," Lindy echoed. She gave him a parting half smile, an accurate reflection of her mixed feelings of gratitude and irritation toward him. He nodded in acknowledgment and turned his back on her.

"Did you have to embarrass me like that?" she said as soon as she and Kevin were out of the sheriff's earshot.

"You, embarrassed? Shoot, Lindy, I didn't think that was possible."

"And did you have to fall all over yourself thanking him? It's his fault I'm late in the first place. He stopped me for speeding and then he impounded my car."

"At least he gave you a ride here," Kevin pointed out.

"He didn't have to do that, and frankly I'm surprised he did. He's a by-the-book kinda guy."

"How do you know him so well?" she asked suspiciously.

"I play poker with him."

They didn't have time for further conversation. The moment they entered the church, Lindy was enveloped by frantic hugs and kisses from her sister and her mother, and various other female relations. Another peach-swathed bridesmaid, Claire's best friend from high school, looked infinitely relieved that she wouldn't have to carry the show alone.

"I'm so glad you made it in time," said Claire as she adjusted her white lace hat, which the hug had knocked askew. "I'd have hated getting married without you as my maid of honor."

Their mother merely rolled her sage-green eyes and shook her head, giving Lindy a look that said, "I can't wait to hear about it."

No one chastised her for cutting it so close.

From inside the patrol car, Thad watched Lindy and Kevin disappear into the church, arm in arm, heads bent together. When the door closed behind them, he put the car in gear and drove away, feeling unaccountably restless, as if he'd left something unfinished.

Three miles out of town, he realized why. He'd written out a traffic citation for Lindy, but he'd neglected to tear it out of the book and give it to her.

The Shapiro-Staples wedding reception was in high gear by the time Thad parked his pickup in the VFW hall's gravel lot. Judging from the vibrations emanating from the hall itself, Pete and the Pit Bulls were letting loose with all the noise their amplifiers could generate.

Though the Shapiros had mailed Thad a bona fide invitation to this shindig, he hadn't planned on coming. He didn't like parties—at least, not those attended by half the county complete with bad C and W music and free-flowing beer. Still, as he'd showered after work and then changed into his civvies, he'd thought of a good reason to attend the reception, after all.

It might even be fun, he mused as he let himself through the heavy double-doors of the cavernous building. There was at least some potential entertainment value in viewing Lindy among her people, in her own element.

Thad had worried that he'd be underdressed for the wedding reception wearing his best jeans, an aqua polo shirt and white linen jacket, but he should have known better. As was normal for this type of event, everyone had changed out of their fancy duds and into more comfortable clothes—everyone except a certain blond bridesmaid.

His eyes were drawn to her immediately. She stood at the hub of activity, a peach-colored flower ringed by a group of beelike admirers enamored with her every word and gesture.

"Hey, Thad, you made it!"

Thad tore his gaze away from Lindy long enough to greet Kevin and endure his well-meaning thump on the shoulder. Kevin had ditched his tux in favor of a white, snap-fronted shirt, a pair of pale blue jeans, and boots that had seen one rodeo too many.

"There's cake and punch that way," Kevin said, pointing toward one end of the hall, "but the good stuff is in the back, where the crowd is."

"Thanks, Kev." Good stuff no doubt meant a keg of Lone Star. From the corner of his eye Thad saw one of Lindy's admirers touch her sleeve and nod toward the dance floor. She responded with a smile and drifted into his arms for an easy waltz.

"She's a sight, isn't she?" Kevin observed with obvious admiration, following Thad's line of vision.

Thad quickly looked away. "Hard to ignore, I'll give her that."

"Did you really threaten to arrest her?"

Just what sort of tales had the woman been spreading? "Sort of," he admitted. "I suppose I did give her a hard time. Under the circumstances, I could have let her go instead of being such a hard-ass."

Kevin laughed. "You never let anyone go. Come on, let's go get some beer."

On the way to the keg they ran into the mother of the bride. "Evening, Judge Shapiro," Thad greeted her, thinking how her frothy green dress made her look less like a judge than usual.

"Oh, Thad, we're not in court here. Call me Marianne." She gave his hand a friendly squeeze as Kevin continued unerringly on his trek toward the keg. "I understand you gave my eldest daughter quite a time this afternoon."

"I guess I did. Sorry about that, Judge—Marianne," he corrected himself. "I hope I didn't cause too much inconvenience."

"Oh, nonsense!" Marianne cut him off as she took him by the arm and led him toward the keg. "I'm sure the incident was entirely her fault, no matter what she says. That girl knows more ways than a half-grown kitten to get herself into trouble. Wouldn't you like a beer, Thad?"

"No, ma'am, I..." He was distracted for a moment as he caught the swirl of a peach-colored skirt in his peripheral vision. She was dancing with a different partner now, and as he watched, another swain cut in and snagged her away. "On second thought, I think I will have something cold," he said, returning his gaze to the judge. "It's been a long, hot day."

"I'll say," Marianne agreed, just as another latecomer at the door claimed her attention. She made sure Thad had a full cup of the cold, foamy brew before excusing herself.

Thad knew many of the wedding guests, and he spent the next twenty minutes caught in a discussion about how to finance the widening of Winthrop Bridge, which ran between Corrigan and Winstonia. All the while he pretended rapt interest in the shrinking tax base, however, another part of his mind was constantly monitoring Lindy Shapiro's progression around the dance floor. Did she ever run out of partners?

He would have approached her when the band took a break, but he found himself paying respects to the bride and groom, whom he knew only slightly. Claire looked a great deal like Lindy, he decided, though she was more petite and her hair was almost a white-blonde, like Kevin's, as opposed to Lindy's head of spun gold.

By the time he'd disentangled himself from an elderly lady and her complaint about the slackly enforced leash laws,

Pete and the Pit Bulls were deep into their deafening performance again and Lindy was locked in the embrace of an older gentleman.

"That's the groom's father," said Kevin from behind Thad's right shoulder, where he'd just materialized. "Are you going to stare at her all night or ask her to dance?"

"Who, me? I wasn't . . . I mean Lindy isn't exactly . . ."

"Isn't exactly *what?*" Kevin stood up straighter and thrust out his chest with the sum total of his protective elder-brotherly instincts.

" . . . My type," Thad finished lamely. "Besides, looks to me like her dance card's filled."

Kevin dismissed Thad's objections with a wave of his hand. "Let me show you how it's done," he said, handing Thad his beer and swaggering out to the dance floor. Within moments the father of the groom had graciously acquiesced so that brother and sister could dance.

Thad continued to watch, fascinated by the easy laughter he saw between the two siblings. Without meaning to, he envisioned himself in Kevin's place, sharing some amusing anecdote with the lithe woman in peach. He could almost feel the soft chiffon of her dress against his hand and smell her delicate fragrance.

He shook his head at his own foolishness. He'd come here for a purpose, and that purpose wasn't to entertain some ridiculous fantasy about himself and the belle of the ball.

With that thought firmly in mind, he set the two cups of beer on an empty table and walked resolutely toward Lindy and Kevin as they weaved in and around the other couples. He caught Kevin's eye first, and gave him a hard stare in lieu of the customary shoulder tap.

"Hey, sis," Kevin said, gently maneuvering Lindy toward Thad, "there's someone else wants to dance with you." With a mischievous grin, he more or less thrust her at Thad and turned tail.

Lindy froze for an instant, astonished by this turn of events, but she recovered quickly and stepped neatly into Thad Halsey's arms. "Well, hello, Sheriff. You know how to two-step?"

"Sure do," he said as he picked up the beat.

For the first time she could remember, Lindy felt awkward dancing. Her attention was consumed by the feel of her hand in Thad's and his light touch at her midriff, so that she kept losing count.

"Relax," he said when she tripped for the third time. Then he pulled her closer and their steps finally smoothed into a comfortable rhythm. Only then did she realize she'd been holding herself away from him as if he were a cactus.

"I hadn't pegged you as the dancing type," she said, her thoughts muddled by his proximity and the provocative scent of his skin. Why was he here? Had he heard some version of the amusing tale she'd told her family about this afternoon's adventure?

"What exactly did you tell your mother about me?" he asked casually, confirming her suspicions.

She squirmed uncomfortably at his steady gaze. "Why, I told the truth, of course... though I might have overdramatized the events just a tad."

"A tad?" he inquired, twirling her around and then back against his chest.

"All right, since Kevin's probably told you anyway, I insinuated that you possess a rattlesnake's compassion and a fence post's sense of humor."

She expected an abrupt end to the dance. Instead, she saw the corner of Thad's mouth twitch almost imperceptibly. "You have a knack for description," was all he said as the dance continued.

She waited, wondering if he would ask for a chance to disprove her misconceptions about him, to get to know her better. But he issued no such invitation.

"Why did you want to dance with me?" she asked, cocking her head to one side.

"Dancing appeared to be the only way I could get your attention," he answered amicably. "And we have some unfinished business."

"We do?"

They stopped dancing. He pulled something from his breast pocket and handed it to her.

She laughed when she recognized the crinkled piece of paper. "My speeding ticket. Did I leave it behind?"

"I never gave it to you."

"And you went to all this trouble to remedy the situation. How...thoughtful. Hey, isn't there some law that says you have to give this thing to me at the scene of the violation?" she teased, determined to pull a smile out of this man.

To her utter surprise he took her seriously. His face turned all hard again and he pointed a finger at her nose. "You're not getting out of paying this ticket, even if your mother *is* the district judge." He turned and strode from the dance floor, giving her little chance to protest her innocence.

Two

___

Thad was in a foul mood when he returned to the office Monday morning. He'd just been to Hazel Ecklund's farm to view the damage to her barn inflicted by a vandal with a can of spray paint.

Normally a little graffiti wasn't cause for alarm. The teenagers in Scanlon County didn't have enough to keep them busy, so they were bound to get out of hand sometimes. Last night, however, some troublemakers had targeted an elderly widow who was barely hanging on to her small chicken farm, and the message they'd scrawled on the side of her barn was quite crude and in full view of everyone who drove past her place.

Hazel had been so distraught that Thad had found himself volunteering to repaint her barn. That wasn't how he'd wanted to spend next weekend, his first full weekend off in longer than he could remember.

His mood didn't improve any when he spotted two of his deputies standing in the lot behind the courthouse, practically drooling over the red Cadillac.

He got out of the patrol car and started through the gate in the chain-link fence, intending to remind them of the reams of paperwork that needed attention, when he spied the Caddy's owner in the driver's seat, demonstrating to her rapt audience the operation of the white canvas top.

"Hey, Sheriff," called out Jimmy McGruder, the younger of the two. He cleared his throat nervously. He was a good kid, but barely out of the police academy and still green as a new stalk of corn. The other deputy, Chet Klingstedt, merely nodded and pursed his lips. He'd been in law enforcement for twenty years or more, and should have known better than to let a pretty blonde lure him away from his duties.

"Well, if it isn't Mr. Law and Order himself," Lindy greeted Thad cheerfully as she popped out of the car. "I didn't know you had Jimmy here working for you. I used to baby-sit him." She put an affectionate arm around Jimmy's thick shoulders and squeezed. "I can't believe he turned into such an upstanding citizen, a deputy, no less. You can't believe the trouble he used to get into."

"Aw, Lindy, cut it out," Jimmy said, turning bright red.

Thad gave both deputies a withering stare. "Don't you boys have work to do?"

"We were just replacing a fuse for Lindy," Chet explained, "so's she could get her car inspected and licensed." He held up a dead fuse as evidence of their dutiful intentions.

"Get on with it, then," Thad said, his words clipped.

"I s'pose we're done now," Chet mumbled. "Everything seems to be working. Come on, Jimmy. You're due in court at eleven. See ya, Lindy."

The two deputies escaped before Thad had further opportunity to chastise them.

Lindy folded her arms across her breasts and leaned back against the car, eyeing Thad with a mutinous expression. "Well, what did I do wrong now?"

He took his time answering. His gaze traveled the length of her, taking in her cropped white T-shirt, snug red shorts and an endless length of tanned legs. "I'd appreciate it," he said slowly, "if you wouldn't spend your free time distracting my deputies. They have more important things to do than stand around staring at your legs."

Her green eyes widened, then narrowed as her slender body stiffened in outrage. "For heaven's sake, Jimmy treats me like an older sister. And you know good and well Chet's eyes are for Eloise only. He's as happily married as a guy can get. In fact, it appears to me, Sheriff, that the only one around here staring at my legs is *you.*"

He started to object that her legs held no interest for him, but she didn't let him interrupt.

"Furthermore, I came here for the sole purpose of paying my ticket and collecting my car. I got my new driver's license this morning, and as soon as the car passes inspection I can come back here and pick up my car tags. And then, thank heaven, I'll be on my way and out of your hair."

"Not quite," he said when she'd finished. "There's a small matter of the impounding fee."

"What? Well, how much is that?"

"Fifty dollars," he answered without blinking. He'd pulled the figure out of thin air.

"Damnation, Sheriff, I don't *have* fifty dollars. My life savings have already gone into the county coffers."

Exactly what he figured. He tried not to let his amusement show. "Guess you'll have to get it from your mother, then," he suggested.

She laughed humorlessly at that. "My family loves me, but not a one of them would lend me a plug nickel. They know me too well for that." She sighed, her brief spurt of anger apparently spent. "Come on, Sheriff, give me a break. You've wiped me out. Waive the fine."

"Where'd you get that ridiculous piece of machinery, anyway?" he asked, ignoring her plea.

"I won it in a radio station contest," she said, her ready smile returning. "You know, it was the strangest thing. I'd just moved to Seattle when my rusty old heap gave up. I went home that night, wondering how I would get to work the next day, when I heard this deejay call out my name on the oldies station. I'd entered the contest the week before. So I called in, and poof, I won a Cadillac. Pretty amazing, huh?"

He nodded, thinking no one should be that lucky. "Amazing, but it doesn't exempt you from the fine."

She made an impatient noise at the back of her throat. "Can I owe it to you?"

"If your own family doesn't give you credit, you think the county should?" Still, he pretended to give her request due consideration. "Around here, when people can't pay their fines, there's another solution."

"And that is?" she asked, raising one skeptical eyebrow.

"Community service. You spend the day working for the county and we'll forget all about that nasty old fine."

He thought she'd balk. Surely she hadn't managed a solid day's work in her whole life, and the prospect should have sent her into a tizzy. Instead, she nodded agreeably. "I can do that. What did you have in mind?"

He didn't suppose a day in bed with the Sheriff constituted community service. The errant thought shocked him so thoroughly he couldn't answer for a moment.

"Well?" she prodded, her hands on her hips in an aggressive stance.

He leaned lower so that their noses were almost touching. "Can you hold a paintbrush?"

Lindy was actually looking forward to her Saturday of "community service." All week long she'd been imprisoned in Kevin's insurance office, filling in for his vacationing secretary. A more physical job suited her better, so a day outdoors in the June sunshine, stretching her muscles, sounded inviting.

The prospect of facing Thad Halsey again gave her only a moment's pause. For some reason he had it in for her. He seemed determined to think the worst of her, and she was just as determined to prove him wrong. True, her family thought her irresponsible, and her smart mouth had been known to get her into scrapes more often than not, but she was basically a decent human being. Perhaps her worst fault was that she hadn't yet discovered what she was good at.

So, okay, by age twenty-six she should at least have a vague idea as to what she wanted to do with her life, but it wasn't as if she hadn't been trying.

She pulled up to the Ecklund place just as the sun was peeking over the trees. Already it was warm and sticky outside. She wished she'd thought to wear a bathing suit under her T-shirt and cutoffs, so she could have caught a few rays. If time permitted, she might take a dip in the inviting creek that ran along the back of the Ecklund property—bathing suit or not.

She parked next to a metallic-blue pickup, got out and walked to the side of the barn to view the damage, but Thad Halsey caught her eye first. He was kneeling on one knee, stirring a five-gallon can of red paint. He looked different in faded-to-white jeans and an old high school basketball jersey—less imposing, certainly. She forced her gaze to the side of the barn, which sported an impromptu hot-pink sign. "Gawd, I'm not sure I even know what all those words mean."

Thad looked up. "Oh, there you are," he said, as if he'd been waiting hours for her.

"Seven-thirty on the dot," she said brightly, wanting to get off to a fresh start with him. "Guess this old barn needed a coat of paint, anyway. Am I supposed to do the whole thing?'' She eyed the acres of weather-beaten siding, thinking how satisfying it would be to see the decrepit building transformed.

''That's the idea. Why don't you get the pans and rollers from the back of my truck. I'll work on the top half, you can do the bottom.''

''You mean you're going to stay and help?'' The idea disturbed her. For some reason, she thought she would have the job to herself.

''Someone has to supervise,'' he replied, tipping up the bill of his baseball cap.

She could have supervised herself, she thought as she went to the truck to fetch the equipment, but she supposed she was grateful to be getting some help, even if it was from the disapproving, stone-faced sheriff.

She opened the tailgate of Thad's pickup, then paused to take a long, uninterrupted look at him. His old jeans bore paint spatters in numerous colors, and his feet were encased in a beat-up pair of high-top basketball shoes. What she could see of his skin was all-over tan, she observed, remembering her curiosity from the other day with a guilty smile. She found herself first admiring his biceps as he hoisted a sixty-foot aluminum ladder into place. Her gaze drifted lower, appreciating his tight buttocks and the strength of his legs beneath the faded denim, as he climbed the ladder to reach the trim around the roof.

''You going to take all day?'' he asked, turning to stare accusingly at her over his shoulder.

Hang you anyway, Thad Halsey! she thought as she quickly gathered up pans, brushes and rollers. See if I ever waste another lustful thought on your worthless hide!

They worked together all morning without speaking. Lindy was determined that, if any conversation was to pass between them, Thad would initiate it. She'd made a friendly overture, after all, and he'd rebuffed her. So she hummed while she painted, figuring that eventually he'd at least have to tell her to shut up, since she knew darn well she was tone deaf. But he remained annoyingly silent.

She put all the energy she had into painting, pausing every so often to survey her progress. But past a certain point the job seemed to be moving more slowly, and the vast expanse still to be covered was daunting. She glanced at her watch. Almost eleven.

She could concentrate on painting for only so long without some distraction. She set down her roller, shaded her eyes and looked toward the top of the ladder, not quite sure what she wanted to say, only that it had to be sensational enough to provoke him.

As if he sensed her eyes on him he looked down while his hand kept up the methodical back-and-forth motion of the brush. "Do you need something?"

"No, I just—Thad, watch out! Watch what you're—" Her warning ended on a gasp as a big wad of twigs and straw sailed past Thad's elbow and fell to the grass below.

"It's just an old bird's nest," he said as she rushed toward the tangled mass.

"No, it's not old," she argued, kneeling to inspect the nest. "I saw the parents flying back and forth to feed the babies. I should have warned you about it." But she'd been too busy pretending she didn't want to talk, she thought with a surge of guilt as she dug gingerly through the destroyed nest in search of life.

Abruptly, four tiny, featherless heads popped up out of the dried twigs as if they all belonged to the same creature. Four mouths gaped open, begging for a meal with piteous little peeps.

Lindy, a childlike sense of wonder on her face, looked up at Thad and smiled delightedly. "Oh, look, they're all right!" she exclaimed.

In that one moment, Thad felt himself soften immeasurably toward his captive labor force. He'd been wrong about her propensity for work—she'd been painting tirelessly all morning, without a single word of complaint. How could he continue to treat her so harshly when she herself held so much compassion for a nestful of pesky sparrows?

He descended the ladder as quickly as he could without falling on his head. "I didn't mean to knock it down," he said, full of remorse as he bent down to have a look at his victims. "I'm sorry. Can you save them? I remember reading somewhere that you shouldn't disturb a fallen nest, that the parent birds will continue to feed the babies no matter where they land."

"But we can't just leave them here," Lindy reasoned. "Sitting in this sun they'll turn into sparrow fricasee. Let's see if we can put the nest back under the eaves. Maybe the parents won't know the difference."

"Won't they smell a human scent on the babies and refuse to feed them?" he asked.

She shrugged. "I don't think sparrows are all that picky." With gentle hands she gathered up the dried mass and held it out to him.

He started to take it, then hesitated. The babies were so tiny and fragile-looking. He was afraid he would hurt them. "How will I hold on to them?" he asked. "I'll need one hand free to climb the ladder."

Lindy pondered the problem for a moment. "I know," she said, putting the nest into his unwilling hands.

He held his breath as she reached for his midsection, unable to fathom her intentions. The gentle contact sent an unwelcome thrill through his body. It was only when she pulled out the hem of his tank shirt and lifted it out in front of him, forming a small hammock with it, that he understood her intent.

"Set the nest in there," she said. He did as directed. She gathered up the hem until the nest was securely suspended. "Hold this in your teeth until you get up there."

I must be out of my mind, he thought as he climbed the ladder with a bird's nest dangling from his teeth. If Lindy wanted to put the nest back under the eaves, why wasn't *she* up here doing it herself? Ah, hell, he might as well abandon that line of thinking. He wanted to save the birds every bit as much as she did.

When he reached the top of the ladder he steadied himself, then scooped the nest out of his shirt and gently tucked it into its former position. It didn't look nearly as secure as it had before, and he didn't believe for a minute that the parent sparrows would be fooled by such a shabby-looking abode, but Lindy undoubtedly had more experience with birds than he did. She'd grown up here, after all, and he was still in many ways a city boy.

Lindy applauded his effort as he came back down the ladder. "Good work, Sheriff," she said.

"Thanks. And you can call me Thad. Want something to drink?" He headed for the cooler he'd brought along in the truck.

"I'd love it. Thad, huh? I don't know. You sure you want to be on a first-name basis with a common criminal like me?"

He turned and handed her a paper cup full of pink lemonade, then poured some for himself. "I guess I have been treating you like a criminal." He took a long sip, letting the cool liquid slide down his parched throat. He hadn't realized how thirsty he was. He'd been waiting for Lindy to insist on a break, but to his surprise she hadn't.

"I don't mind taking my licks when I deserve them," she said, wiping her face with a bandanna she'd tied around her neck. "I'll pay my speeding tickets, I'll pay the licensing and inspection fees, and I'll even paint the barn, but I don't see why I should be forced to endure your unpleasantness. Have you singled me out, or do you treat everyone this way?"

Directly confronted in such an open manner, Thad didn't have a lot to say in his own defense. Fortunately he didn't have to. A short, hefty bundle of energy was trundling toward them from the house, creating a good distraction. Hazel Ecklund, clad in a green-checked apron and carrying a big cardboard box, smiled a greeting.

Thad met her halfway, relieving her of the box. "What's this?"

"It's lunch, what else?" she answered. "I seen you and your helper taking a break, and I figured it was time to bring on some chow."

"You didn't have to do that, Mrs. Ecklund," Thad protested, though he was already lifting the foil back on the various dishes in the box. Fried chicken, barbecued beans and fresh peach cobbler. He'd died and gone to heaven.

"Nonsense." She surveyed the barn with a delighted cackle. "You're doing a terrific job, just wonderful. My old barn'll be so spiffy that my chicken house and fence will look positively shabby. If I could just get my son to put a little work into—why Lindy Shapiro, if my eyes don't deceive me!"

"Hey, Mrs. Ecklund," Lindy said, giving the old woman a hug.

"When did you get back in town?"

"Just about a week ago," she answered. "For Claire's wedding, but I think I'll stick around awhile."

Was there anyone in town who didn't know Lindy? Thad wondered.

"You'll have to stop by for some eggs before you leave. Oh, and I have a new batch of baby chicks you just have to see, all fuzzy and yellow. You might be able to talk me out of one if you play your cards right." She winked. "Gracious, it's hot out here. I'd better get back inside before I roast. You can just leave the dishes in the barn, and I'll fetch 'em later." She turned and waddled away as Lindy and Thad exchanged a meaningful look.

"She used to give me chicks as pets," Lindy explained as they drifted toward the barn's invitingly shady interior. "I'd

raise them in my room until they got to be too big and
clucky, or until they started trying to nest in the linen closet
or crow at four o'clock in the morning. Then Mom would
get on my case, and I'd trade the big chicken in on a new
little one. Mrs. Ecklund claimed that the hens I raised were
more productive."

"I'll bet they were," Thad agreed wryly. Lindy probably
charmed the eggs right out of them.

"So, what brought you to Scanlon County?" she asked
as they settled onto some old hay bales, the lunch box between them. She reached inside and pulled out two plates,
forks, and a handful of paper napkins.

"A want ad," he confessed. "I was fed up with the big-
city police treadmill. I saw an ad for a small-town deputy in
a trade magazine, I applied for the job, and I got it. A year
later I ran for sheriff and won."

"Do you like it?" she asked.

"Sure I do." He took a bite out of a crispy drumstick and
nodded appreciatively. "It's exactly the sort of job I knew
I'd end up with some day. What about you? Why are you
back in Corrigan? How long have you been gone, anyway?"

"I haven't lived here full-time since I went away to school.
That was, gosh, eight years ago. Hard to believe." She bit
into a juicy thigh. "Mmm, Hazel fries the best chicken. For
years I couldn't eat any that came from her farm. I thought
it might be...you know. One of my pets."

He grimaced at the thought. "So where'd you go to
school?" he asked.

"Well, Texas A & M for a couple of years. Then I transferred to Rice for one year, then University of Texas, then,
let's see—oh, yeah, SMU for one semester but it was too
expensive, so I switched to Baylor—"

"Good Lord, were you trying to cover the entire South-
west Conference?"

She shrugged. "I was just trying to graduate. I must have racked up enough hours to get a doctorate. Problem is, I never took enough hours in any one subject to earn even a bachelor's. I switched majors a lot."

Thad suspected that was an understatement.

They were silent for a few minutes as they put a hefty dent in the food supply, but it wasn't the tense silence that had gripped them throughout the morning.

"So when you weren't going to school, what did you do?" he asked after he'd served up two messy squares of cobbler.

"I worked, and I traveled. I prospected for gold in Nevada, but I didn't find anything. I cleaned fish tanks at the aquarium in San Francisco. I was a nanny for a nice family in Boston—they took me on vacation with them, so I got to spend a couple of months in France. My last job I was a harbor tour guide in Seattle."

"Didn't it work out?"

"It did until my roommate fell in love with a musician and kicked me out so the guy could move in with her. That's when I decided to come home for a while. I was starting to miss my family. I could hardly remember Claire as anything more than a pigtailed brat, and here she was getting married. It blew my mind."

"How long do you think you'll stay?"

"Why? You can't wait to be rid of me, right? You're afraid I'll unsettle your nice, settled little town?"

That's exactly what he feared. Or, more accurately, that she'd unsettle his nice, safe, uncomplicated life. She'd already caused him to do and say some rather peculiar things. "I'm just politely curious, that's all," he answered her.

"I'll stay until I feel like leaving again," she said. A simple, direct answer that left Thad completely dissatisfied.

They fed their leftovers to a skinny barn cat, then packed up the box and left it in the barn as Hazel had directed.

"So, how long a lunch break does the prison laborer get?" Lindy asked. "Can I take an extra fifteen minutes for a quick dip in the creek?"

"Uh, Lindy, there's something I ought to tell you," Thad said, hating himself for what he was about to confess. "I, um, sort of made you come here under false pretenses."

"You *what?*"

"There was no impounding charge. I made it up. You can leave if you want. Hell, I'll even pay you for the work you put in this morning."

She was so astonished at Thad's admission she didn't know what to say. She ought to be angry—no, *furious*. But all she could manage was an overwhelming need to know what would make him do such a thing. "Why?" she asked.

He hesitated. "I'm not sure. Maybe it's because you struck me as the kind of person who skates through life, the kind nothing bad ever happens to because you're cute and clever, and everyone lets you get away with murder."

She chewed on her lower lip for a few moments, puzzling out what he'd said. "I do skate through life, I guess," she said. "I'm lucky. I manage to land on my feet more often than not. What's so wrong about that?"

"Ah, hell, I don't know. I just think people should face the consequences of their actions, that's all." He sounded unbearably pompous, even to his own ears.

"But you made up consequences that didn't even exist."

"I know, and I'm sorry. I don't know what got into me. Normally I'm not—" His attention wavered as his eyes followed something behind Lindy. She turned and immediately saw what had so captivated him. Mama sparrow was flying toward the nest with a piece of straw trailing from her beak. As they watched, she wove the straw into the formless nest and began to tidy it up. Soon Papa sparrow joined her with a piece of something in his mouth. Judging from the excited peeps, he was feeding the babies.

"Well, I'll be damned," Thad said in a hushed voice.

Lindy tore her gaze away from the birds long enough to look at him. What she saw brought her heart into her throat. A bunch of stupid sparrows had done what she couldn't.

Sheriff Thad Halsey was smiling.

"You should do that more often," she said, touching the corner of his mouth with her forefinger. "You're downright irresistible-looking when you smile." She stood on tiptoe and pressed her lips where her finger had just touched.

The noon sun's intensity was nothing compared to the heat that flooded her body when she felt his skin against her mouth. She pulled away quickly, aghast at what she'd done.

He made no reaction, other than to stare at her quizzically. He was still smiling, although the mood he reflected now was less exuberant, more curious.

She had to get away before she said or did anything else stupid. Gawd, she simply had to learn to control her impulsiveness! "The creek," she said, her words a mere gurgle. "I'm going for a swim."

She turned and bolted.

Even yards away from him, her insides simmered from his remembered nearness, and the jubilation his smile had brought. One smile, and it seemed as if his whole personality had changed. He wasn't really a stuffy, overconscientious tyrant. He was a sensitive, caring man who could smile over the triumph of a nestful of tiny, insignificant sparrows. She might even find he had a sense of humor, if she dug deep enough. No telling what sorts of wonderful qualities he was hiding behind that taciturn mask.

With a flash of incredible insight, she realized why the Fates had brought her back home. She was here to reveal the man behind the brick wall.

Three

———

Somehow Lindy muddled through the remainder of the afternoon. She could have abandoned the project, since the sheriff had sprung her loose, but for once she felt a certain obligation to finish what she'd started.

Still, after she'd returned from wading in the creek—there wasn't enough water to actually swim—she hadn't felt ready to face him or the desire she'd unwittingly stirred up. By some mutual, unspoken agreement they had split up, with Lindy working on one side of the barn and Thad on the other, completely out of sight of each other.

It was only toward sunset that their paths began to converge on the fourth wall.

Thad gave an elaborate sigh from his perch on the ladder. "We're almost done," he announced.

"Looks that way," Lindy agreed, risking a glance upward. He'd taken off his shirt. The muscles on his back were firmly delineated, and they rippled with each stroke of the paintbrush.

"Hazel's right," he said. "Now that the barn's painted, the rest of the place looks run down."

Lindy tore her eyes away from his delectable body to have a look at the Ecklund property. The main house desperately needed a new roof, a coat of paint and some windows replaced. The chicken coop looked like it was about to collapse. The fence sagged, and the grass needed mowing. She remembered that years ago, the place had been beautifully maintained.

"Needs a lot of work, all right," she said. "Hazel isn't making ends meet since Hank died, is she?"

"Nope. She can't unload this inflated land they bought ten years ago."

Lindy turned her attention back to the barn. Thad had made a few rough repairs to the structure, in addition to the paint. "I'm glad we could do this for her," she said. "Neighbors ought to help each other, like in the old days. I mean, how long has it been since this area's seen a good old-fashioned barn raising?"

"Not since before I moved here," Thad replied as he descended the ladder. "You know, we aren't going to finish this today."

"A couple more hours in the morning ought to take care of it," she ventured.

"I'll finish it up. There's no need for you to come back out."

Lindy couldn't tell whether he was just being nice, or he really didn't care for her company. Either way, she felt inclined to argue with him. "I'd like to see it finished," she said.

"There's really no need," Thad insisted. He should have welcomed her help, but frankly, he wasn't sure how much more of her he could take. Ever since she'd kissed him—a mere peck on the cheek—he hadn't been able to keep his mind on painting. She'd come back from the creek with her pink T-shirt clinging to her damp skin, plainly revealing her braless state. Her breasts were on the small side, he'd noticed. Why, then, had he experienced a rush of lust so consuming he'd lost his sanity for a moment and stepped right into an empty paint can? Thankfully she hadn't seen him do it.

Throughout the afternoon, just the knowledge that she was on the other side of the barn had sent his blood rushing around trying to put out the fire. Finally, he'd vowed not to look at her again until the sun had dried out her shirt.

All right, so he was attracted to her. He had been all along, but now he was forced to admit it. That didn't mean he had to do anything about it. Removing her from his presence ought to ensure that he wouldn't.

"So, do you have anything exciting planned for the rest of the weekend?" Lindy asked casually as they washed their brushes, rollers and pans at the old-fashioned pump.

"I'm planning to clean out my garage," he replied, watching the water sluice over her small, capable hands. "If I have time, I'll waterproof my dock."

Her hands stilled as her forehead wrinkled in apparent concentration. "How will you stand the excitement?"

He raised one wry eyebrow, but refused to be baited.

"Seriously, don't you want to relax after all this hard work?"

He shrugged. "For me, taking care of things at home is relaxing."

"What do you do about dinner?"

"Oh, I'll probably throw a steak on the grill. Why? What are your big plans?"

"Nothing all that big, really. A group of us are going dancing at Tee-Jay's. I've been filling in all week for Kevin's secretary, so as a reward he's promised to buy me all the beer I can drink." She laughed at the look Thad gave her. "Don't worry, it's a pretty safe promise, seeing as I don't drink beer. I mostly just go there to dance. You're welcome to join us."

He shook his head as they loaded the equipment into the back of his truck. "Thanks, but no. I have to confess—though I've adapted to most of the small-town trappings around here, country music isn't too high on my list of favorite things."

"But you two-step just fine," she objected.

"It's not all that difficult...." He glanced nervously at his watch. "Listen, I really have to, um, get home. Thanks for your help." Abruptly he turned away from her, climbed into the truck and slammed the door.

"Yup, don't want to keep that garage waiting," Lindy murmured as she watched him drive away. She couldn't help feeling a little disappointed. Thad had greeted her invitation with the enthusiasm he might reserve for a rattlesnake barbecue.

That's what she got for trying to be friendly, she thought as she slipped behind the wheel of the Caddy. Still, she wasn't ready to give up on Thad Halsey. Not by a long shot. She couldn't allow all those good looks to go to waste on dirty garages and weather-worn docks. Someone ought to teach the man how to have fun, and it might as well be her.

When Lindy and Kevin arrived at Tee-Jay's around ten that night, the place was jumping. A group of their old high-school friends was already there, kicking up sawdust on the dance floor.

Lindy found a seat at one of the long tables, ordered a root beer from the waitress, and settled back to watch the shenanigans. Immediately she received several invitations to dance, which she turned down with a smile. She wasn't really in the mood to dance, she decided.

It didn't take long for Kevin to notice this aberration in her behavior. "What's wrong with you, sis?" he asked, plopping down in the chair next to hers. "Don't you like the band?"

"Oh, they're okay," she replied. "I guess I'm just pooped. Twelve straight hours painting is enough to do in anybody." She massaged her upper arm for emphasis. By tomorrow she'd probably need horse linament for her sore muscles.

"I still can't believe the trick Halsey played on you," Kevin said, laughing. "You must have been mad enough to spit."

"You can say that again." That wasn't exactly the truth, but she didn't see the point in explaining to Kevin that, more than anything, she'd been hurt to discover what a low opinion of her Thad held.

"I guess that squelches any possible romantic notions he might have had."

"What?" she asked sharply. "What are you talking about?"

"Oh, nothing really. Just the way he was staring at you during the reception. I thought maybe you'd fired a spark plug in him, but I guess not."

"He was staring at me?"

"Constantly." Kevin shrugged and took another swig of beer.

"If he was, it wasn't because he's interested, that's for sure. I asked him if he wanted to join us tonight, and he turned me down. Flatter than a pancake. Couldn't escape fast enough."

Kevin sat up straighter, eyeing his sister speculatively. "That's a new experience for you, isn't it?"

"What?"

"Getting turned down. I don't recall it's ever happened before. Why, back in high school you had every guy—"

"Oh, Kevin, this isn't high school. And believe me, I'm no stranger to rejection."

He leaned back and gave her a teasing smile, but then turned serious. "It's just as well you two don't get together."

"Why do you say that?" she asked, slightly miffed.

"Because, Thad's a nice guy. A little stiff and formal, sometimes, but—"

"Now just a damn minute!" Lindy objected. "Are you saying I'm not nice enough for him?"

"Well..." Kevin hesitated. "It's not that, exactly. But let's face it, sis, you've dated just about every eligible man in the county at one time or another. And you've blown them all off, too. You're fickle, and you know it."

She opened her mouth to protest, then stopped. He was right. Of course, all Kevin had to go on were her high school antics, and the few summers since then that she'd spent in Corrigan, but her romance track record hadn't improved any. Two months was the longest she'd ever dated anyone. "I don't do it on purpose," she said, knowing it was a feeble defense. "I'm not deliberately hateful."

"I know." He pulled a lock of her hair, the way he'd teased her since they were children. "Still, I'd hate to see you trample on Thad's ego. You don't really know him. He's a very serious, very intense person. He hasn't had an easy life. If he started going out with you, he wouldn't take it lightly."

She rolled her eyes.

"I mean it, Lindy. When you got tired of him, tired of Corrigan, and you jumped up and moved to Timbuktu or wherever, he wouldn't take that lightly, either."

She gave a short laugh that sounded brittle to her own ears. "Don't sweat it, Kev. The sheriff and I are as different as...as this place is to Buckingham Palace. I doubt we'd last through a single date."

Kevin shook his head, smiling enigmatically.

It was a blazing-hot Fourth of July, more than a week after the barn-painting, when Thad saw Lindy again. Corrigan was in the throes of its annual Independence Day celebration, complete with a chili cook-off, a watermelon-seed-spitting contest, and an armadillo race. As in many years past, the Sheriff's Department had been called in to help out with security.

As Thad ambled through the crowd, watching the home-spun parade, he idly wished he wasn't on duty. For once he might like to enjoy the festivities instead of keeping his guard up all day. Hardly more than a handful of people around here knew him in anything other than his official capacity. They were polite but wary, as if they expected him to spoil their fun.

Perhaps they were right. Some kids were already setting off bottle rockets, and he had the unpopular duty of trying to stop them. Fireworks were illegal within the city limits and a real danger in a crowd this size.

He heard a telltale hiss and pop, about two blocks north of his current position—probably in the alley behind the hardware store. The fire bugs always managed to stay one step ahead of him.

He increased his pace to a brisk walk, intending to catch the troublemakers in the act this time, when something in the parade caught his eye. Right behind the Girl Scouts' float came Lindy's red convertible, bearing a long paper banner that read Corrigan High Homecoming Queens, Past and Present. Kevin Shapiro sat behind the wheel, grinning ear to ear.

Thad dismissed the illegal fireworks for the moment and gave the parade his full attention. Six women of varying ages, from a teenager to a septuagenarian, were crowded into the Cadillac. They all wore rhinestone tiaras and sashes bearing the year of their reign. He wasn't too surprised to see Lindy sitting in the middle of them, looking more mis-chievous than regal in a Hawaiian-print sundress.

A homecoming queen. That figured.

She smiled and waved—not the stiff, beauty queen's smile, but one of genuine enjoyment—and every so often she threw a handful of chocolate doubloons into the crowd.

Thad felt his chest tighten as she flashed that smile in his direction. She seemed to hold something special in her expression, something just for him.

"Hey, Sheriff, catch!" she called out as she tossed some candy his way. Involuntarily he reached up and snatched a doubloon out of the air as the onlookers around him scrambled for the rest. Pleased with his eye-hand coordination, he tucked his prize into his shirt pocket. When he looked up again she'd passed him and was smiling at someone else.

The brief encounter left him feeling vaguely cheated. Or maybe just foolish, for letting her get to him like that. He pulled the chocolate morsel out of his pocket, unwrapped it and popped it into his mouth when no one was looking.

The rest of the day he kept expecting to run into Lindy. He'd see the flash of Hawaiian print coming around a corner and brace himself for the confrontation, only to realize the print belonged to a stranger's dress or shirt.

As dusk fell and a band began tuning up for a street dance, he concluded that she must have gone home and decided it was just as well. He was on duty, and she'd be an unwelcome distraction.

Just as his traitorous mind began to elaborate on how she might distract him, he stumbled right into the middle of a boisterous group of teenagers in a parking lot. There was no disguising their activity; they'd just ignited a Roman candle. These kids had eluded him all day, and now that he had them, he intended to give them a good talking-to—scare a little respect for the law into them.

But they must have sensed the impending presence of authority, because before he'd taken two steps toward them they'd scattered—all but the one who clutched the spewing plastic cone in her hand. And she was no teenager, Thad soon realized with a jolt.

Lindy held the candle out from her body, her face turned away from the flashes and her eyes clenched shut. Someone had to supervise these little delinquents, she thought, or they'd burn down the whole town. But really, she didn't mind. She loved fireworks—not so much the way they looked, but the excitement of igniting them, of waiting for the whoosh and the flash and the bang.

"Is it done yet?" she asked when the pops and fizzles diminished.

"I'd say so," a deep voice answered.

Her eyes flew open. "Thad! What are you...where'd everyone go?"

He gave her his best granite face. "Kids I can understand. But Lindy, you're old enough to know better than to set off fireworks in the city." He reached into his back pocket.

"This isn't what it looks like. I was only—hey, wait a minute, you aren't writing me a ticket, are you?" she said when she realized he was furiously printing in his citation book.

"What do you think?"

"You aren't even going to let me explain?"

He nodded toward the spent cone in her hand. "Caught you red-handed."

"Thad, no one enforces the fireworks law on Fourth of July. People have been setting them off all day."

"And I've been trying to stop them all day." He tore the citation out of the book and handed it to her.

She snatched it away from him and stuffed it into the pocket of her dress as he turned and started to walk away. "Now, just a damn minute," she said as she followed, trotting to keep up with his long-legged, determined stride. "I'll pay the stupid ticket, but you could at least listen to what I have to say. I was just—" She grabbed his arm and jerked him to a stop. "Will you listen?"

He gave a resigned huff. "All right, I'm listening," he said, tapping his polished boot on the pavement.

"What is it with you? What do you have against me? I've been a pretty good sport about this. I could have put up a fuss about painting that barn, but I didn't. In fact, I thought we were starting to sort of get along, but it seems we're back to square one!"

"I can't help it if you keep breaking the law," he said.

"Technically, yes. But when I saw the stash of fireworks those kids had, I knew they were determined to set them off and nothing I could say would have stopped them. So I asked if I could come along. I figured at least that way I could keep an eye on them and make sure they were doing it safely."

"You call holding a Roman candle in your hand safe?" Thad countered.

"Oh, lighten up, would you? That wasn't even a real Roman candle. It was more like a big sparkler."

"You aren't exactly setting a sterling example, you know. The juvenile delinquency problem in this area—"

"Please, you don't have to lecture. All the so-called civic leaders are always spouting off about this terrible delinquency problem, but how many of them are willing to spend time with the kids, to just talk to them, enjoy them? When was the last time you spent a few minutes with some kids? At least I do that."

The foot-tapping stopped and he lowered his eyes. Obviously her barb had found its mark. "All right, you've made your point. Give me back the ticket."

"Oh, I'll pay the fine, and I'll make sure my chicken-hearted little friends pay their share. If I weaseled out of it, that *would* set a bad example. That's really not the issue."

He looked up, his mood changing swiftly from one of guilt to one of challenge. "Oh? And what is the issue?"

"Why you're picking on me. And I think I know the answer."

"You do, huh?" He folded his arms and cocked his hips in a timeless stance of male bravado.

"You're picking on me because you're jealous. You're jealous because I know how to have fun and you don't. You try to spoil my fun by making me miserable, but I won't let you, and that makes you even madder."

He stared at her in disbelief. "That's lunacy. In the first place, I'm not picking on you. In the second place, I do too know how to have fun."

She shook her head. "I've been watching you. You stroll around this place like a Gestapo soldier guarding a prison camp, on the lookout for an escapee. Why don't you relax and enjoy it?"

"I am enjoying it," he insisted, still focused on the fact that she'd been watching him. How had he missed that?

"Hah. Prove it." She looked around pensively, eventually locking her gaze on a huge plastic bubble set up in the middle of the street. "Do the Moon Walk with me."

"What?" He had to raise his voice to be heard over the band, which had just begun to play in earnest.

"Any adult who enters a Moon Walk knows how to have fun. Come on. Be impulsive for a change." She grabbed his big hand in her small one and led him toward the bubble, which quivered like a mound of gelatin as its small occupants jumped around inside.

He balked. "I can't do this. I'm on duty."

"Oh, phooey. That's just an excuse. The Corrigan police chief is on duty, and look—he's dancing." She pointed to the portly, middle-aged man in uniform who was engaged in a lively two-step with his wife.

"That's different," Thad argued. "A guy can dance without completely undermining his dignity."

"Good, then we'll dance." Still holding his hand, she led him toward the loosely knit crowd of street dancers, pleased at how neatly she'd trapped him.

Thad knew he'd been hornswoggled. He thought about putting up a struggle, until he decided this wasn't such a bad deal, after all. The band was a definite cut above the Pit

Bulls, and it had just struck up the "Orange Blossom Special," a more-than-tolerable bluegrass tune.

"Can you polka?" Lindy asked.

In answer he swept her up, quickly proving his proficiency. The lively music propelled them across the pavement at breakneck speed. They deftly skirted slower couples, dodging empty beer cans on the ground with equal ease as their movements coordinated in perfect harmony. They kept up the breathless pace until their surroundings became nothing but a blur and Lindy was laughing giddily.

Her laughter was almost a tangible thing, tickling Thad's senses like a feather duster. Spurred by her enjoyment, he put even more energy into the dance and twirled her toward the fringes of the group. A few steps more and they were far away from the stage lights, with the twilight shadows enveloping them.

At last the strains of the fiddles faded into the night and the crowd broke into applause. Still, he didn't release her. A wildness beat inside him, an uncontrollable seed of craziness trying to take root. Her body felt warm and firm next to his, and he couldn't bring himself to let her go.

"Where *did* you learn how to dance?" Lindy asked breathlessly, staring up at him with a flushed face and her hair woven in and around itself in a tousled mop.

Instead of answering her, he gathered her closer and captured her startled mouth with his. The surprise lasted only a moment, and then Lindy melted into the kiss, as warm as butter in the sun.

Impossible, Thad's mind chanted even as his lips moved hungrily over hers. How had they gone from arguing over fireworks to dancing to kissing in such a short span of time?

Then he ceased to think at all.

She greeted the bold thrust of his tongue with a quiet moan, for his ears only, and wrapped her arms more tightly around his neck, pulling him still closer. He slid his palm upward from the small of her back, between her shoulder blades, and to the nape of her neck, amazed at the firmness of her muscles and at how pleasing they were to the touch. Her thick, soft hair tickled the back of his hand.

He ended the kiss only because he knew he would pass out if he didn't breathe. Gasping in unison, they stood staring at each other for an eternity, neither of them speaking.

It took Thad a long moment to realize the full import of what he'd just done. He'd been making out with the district judge's daughter, in full view of anyone who'd cared to look. Had he completely lost his mind? Automatically he eased his body away from hers as his eyes darted to the left, then the right.

"No one's paying the slightest bit of attention to us," she said, reading him like a billboard. "So don't spoil it by getting all nervous."

He sighed. "Lindy, I didn't mean to—"

"And don't apologize! I asked for impulsiveness and I got it. A good, healthy display of it, I might add."

Unsure what to make of her mood, he took her hand and guided her down the street, farther away from the raucous music. He would have liked to tell her how exotic she looked, and how soft the skin at the back of her neck had felt against his palm, and how she always smelled like some kind of delicate flower. But such sentiments would have pulled him even deeper into the hole he'd just dug for himself.

They found themselves walking through the grammar school playground. They paused by the massive stone drinking fountain for a sip of lukewarm water as the silence stretched between them like a slingshot.

"I'm not very good with words, Lindy," he finally said. "But I'll give this a try, because I couldn't kiss a woman like that and then walk away without an explanation."

"But you don't have to—"

"The truth is you utterly fascinate me." He plowed on despite her protest. "I tried to simply write you off as a

flake, but I know there's more to you than meets the eye."
He didn't tell her the most significant thing—that she
awakened elements of him he hadn't known were there.
Whenever she was around, he felt a certain awareness that
was exciting, yet disturbing. He wasn't ready to deal with it.

"So what are you saying?" she asked. "You want to get
to know me better?"

"No. I want you to stay away from me." The words actually caused her to flinch, and he knew then he was handling everything wrong.

"Why?" she asked.

Choking out the next few words was one of the hardest
things he'd ever faced. "Lindy, I can't get involved with
you. Even friendship would be a risky undertaking."

"Wait a minute. You just said I was fascinating."

"You're also a virtual advertisement for trouble. I have
a feeling that when it finds you, somehow I'll be in the
middle of it and you'll slip out of it unscathed and move on
to your next adventure, leaving the mess for me to clean up."

She stared at him, hardly able to believe he could say
something so outrageous, and right to her face. She was so
mad she wanted to throw something at him, or at the very
least slap that martyred, self-righteous look off his handsome face.

"You really are a by-the-book kinda guy, aren't you,
Sheriff?" she asked when she was calm enough to speak.
"That's how Kevin describes you. Have you ever once taken
a chance on something? Have you ever done something just
for the hell of it?"

"That's not my way," he said. "Maybe it's the responsibility that goes with my job, I don't know."

She seemed to consider that for a moment. When she
spoke again, her eyes were as hard as fine emeralds. "Maybe
I am trouble, but at least I'm enjoying life. Wish I could say
the same for you."

She turned swiftly away from him, but he grabbed her arm and stopped her before she could get very far. "Lindy, please understand. I've worked too hard for my little slice of contentment. I can't risk losing that—I can't."

The fire seemed to go out of her. "Contentment? I guess that's enough—for some people." She pulled loose of his grasp.

This time he let her walk away.

Four

The sun, a bright orange ball, had just touched the glassy surface of Arrowrock Lake, spilling its last rays over the smooth waters. Thad lay in a hammock in his backyard with a beer in his hand and gazed out into the still, mid-July evening, waiting to experience the sense of satisfaction that always claimed him at times like this.

It didn't come.

He had everything he'd ever wanted. His small lakefront house, with its neat green lawn and tall oak trees, was the sort of home he'd once dreamed of—a far cry from the claustrophobic brick and concrete of his urban childhood. He had a job he enjoyed, one that made him feel useful and gave him a sense of belonging in the community.

People respected him. He respected himself. Given his upbringing—no father and a mother who didn't give a damn what he did—he knew he'd beaten incredible odds by even finishing high school. He'd pushed himself through the police academy and had graduated at the top of his class. He was proud of everything he'd accomplished.

But he wasn't satisfied, dammit. Not anymore.

It was all Lindy Shapiro's fault. Her words were the ones that had taunted him all week, during any unguarded moment, during sleepless hours at night. *Contentment. That might be enough—for some people.*

When had he stopped reaching? he wondered. When had he gotten so lazy that he'd stopped setting goals and declared himself content? Maybe he was content, but he wasn't happy. He'd lost that giddy sense of accomplishment that came with achievement. He was no longer moving forward. His life was stagnant . . . dull.

An outsider might look at the situation and come up with a simple solution: he needed a family. That was the next logical step in his life. But Thad would have to disagree. After all, the family he started out with had been more of a detriment than an asset. He had gotten along just fine without close familial ties, and he had no intention of changing the status quo. At thirty-two he'd been on his own, relied on himself, for too many years.

If not family, then what? Where could he find a new challenge to get his blood pumping again?

The beer had grown warm in his hand. He hadn't taken even one sip. Disgusted, he poured the gold-colored liquid onto the grass and flung the empty can up onto the deck.

Maybe he needed some exercise. The relentless Texas summer heat had forced him to cut back on his workouts; perhaps that was why he felt so restless.

Five minutes later, he found himself pedaling his tenspeed across Winthrop Bridge toward Corrigan. Now that daylight was fading, the wind blowing against his face was cooling down. He concentrated on the pleasant feeling of stretching out muscles and working his lungs and heart.

He intended to ride to the high school, run a couple of miles around the football field track, and ride back. After

a workout like that, he figured, sheer exhaustion would keep
all disturbing thoughts at bay. Of course, even in sleep he
wasn't home free. When Lindy's words weren't taunting
him, images of her sleek body invaded his dreams.

Somehow he never made it to the school. He ended up
wandering aimlessly through one of Corrigan's sleepy resi-
dential neighborhoods instead. Or maybe not so aimlessly,
he realized as he coasted slowly past Judge Shapiro's home.

The house was a stately brick colonial on a large, heavily
wooded lot with a circular drive. Thad slowed his bike to a
crawl and gazed at the warm lights that glowed from within.
Something tugged at him, tugged at the handlebars of his
bike, trying to get him to turn toward the house. He resisted, gliding past and on to the end of the street.

He went around the block three times before his good
sense deserted him and he veered into the driveway. He
didn't stop at the front door, but rode around to the back.
The red Cadillac was parked at a decidedly crooked angle on
a cement pad next to the detached garage, as if the driver
hadn't bothered to take the time to straighten it up.

She probably hadn't, Thad mused with a shake of his
head.

A light shone through a window from the apartment
above the garage. Last night at their weekly poker game,
Kevin had mentioned that's where she was staying for the
summer. Strains of rock music drifted downward, plainly
discernible even over the clattering of an old air-conditioner
in the window.

It was too late to be making unannounced visits—almost
dark, in fact. He should turn around and ride home. Instead, he dismounted and leaned the bike against the garage wall. The pull on him now had a name, and it was
impossible to resist. He took the creaky wooden staircase
two steps at a time, then knocked briskly on the garage
apartment's door.

Lindy looked up sharply when the knock sounded. "Just a minute," she called out. With a frustrated sigh she transferred a long, torpid snake from her lap to a box on the floor. The reptile was still breathing, but it had hardly moved an inch since she'd rescued it from certain death a few hours ago.

She stood to turn down the music and answer the knock.

The last person she'd expected to see standing outside her door at nine o'clock on a Thursday night was Thad Halsey. In truth, she hadn't expected to see him anyplace, at any time. Not after the words they'd flung at each other.

"Hey, Sheriff," she said as she opened the screen door and carelessly gestured for him to enter. She struggled to look and sound indifferent, though the sight of him made her feel anything but. She still smarted from the way he'd dismissed her the last time she'd seen him, but her resentment warred with another, more potent feeling that had her wanting to reach a hand out and touch that warm, tanned skin.

"So, what law did I break this time?" she asked when he didn't jump to explain his presence.

He didn't rise to the bait, as she thought he would. When he finally raised his gaze to meet hers, he appeared distinctly uneasy. "Could I have a glass of water?"

"I suppose I could manage that," she replied coolly, grateful for an excuse to disappear into the kitchen for a moment. As she cracked open a tray full of ice cubes and dumped them into a jelly jar glass, she struggled to get a firm hold on herself.

Damned if he wasn't tanned all over, she thought, glancing through the doorway at his muscular legs revealed so fetchingly by a pair of skimpy athletic shorts. But she refused to let a good tan and a spectacular bod sway her. He had nerve, showing up here after he'd told *her* to stay away from *him*, and she wouldn't forgive him easily. Her pride was at stake.

She returned to the living room and wordlessly handed him the ice water. He downed the whole thing in a series of gulps while she watched in frank fascination. Never had a hot, winded man looked so touchable. Stroking her pride wouldn't give her near as much pleasure as stroking Thad's biceps would.

He set the glass on her coffee table. "I rode my bike—didn't realize how hot it was."

"All the way from Winstonia?"

He shook his head. "I live about halfway between here and there, near the dam."

She figured that was still a good seven or eight miles. "You're into long-distance riding, then?" she asked, thinking how ludicrous it was that they were having this stupid conversation about cycling when what she really wanted to know was why he'd come in the first place.

"I bike or run when I can, and I want to talk about what happened the other day."

It took her a few moments to assimilate the two incongruous thoughts he'd just strung together. Then she folded her arms and responded in kind. "I prefer swimming, myself...and which part do you want to talk about? The fireworks citation, the kiss, or the part where you told me to get lost?"

"The last part," he said with a grimace as he started to pace the small room. "You tried to tell me something then, and I wasn't listening."

"Oh." Try as she might, she couldn't remember what she'd said that night. She only remembered the emotions behind the words—the anger, the outrage. And the kiss. Her memory of the kiss was good and clear. She recalled the exact feel of his mouth on hers, his hands on her back and in her hair. She'd relived it a hundred times. "Maybe you should sit down," she said, but the advice was better taken by herself than him. She sank into the faded plaid couch, indicating that he should take the yellow chair across from her. "Now, refresh my memory," she said, more calmly than she would have thought possible. "Exactly what did we discuss?"

"My life. How I don't take risks and I don't have fun. You might have a point."

Now it was coming back to her, and she was slightly alarmed that he'd taken her careless words at face value. "Ah, hell, Sheriff, I just popped off the first smart one-liner that came into my head. You weren't supposed to go and reevaluate your whole life because of it."

"But I did, and I'm not sure I liked what I saw."

She paused, letting that sink in. Her gaze drifted around the room, trying to see her tiny apartment through his eyes. The furniture was old and the walls needed a coat of paint. Maybe she ought to fix it up a bit, hang a few pictures—even if she was only here for the summer.

"So," she said after a few uncomfortable moments of silence, "are you planning to liven up your life? Thinking of taking up skydiving, perhaps?"

"I had something a little more exciting in mind." The look he gave her made her skin tingle. Abruptly he stood, picked up his glass and headed for her kitchen. "You don't mind if I refill this, do you?"

"No," she answered quietly. She heard the water running. Involuntarily she stood and followed him. "Are you going to elaborate?"

He took another long draft of water before answering. "Stands to reason, if I want to learn how to have fun, to take risks, I ought to learn from the best, right?"

Was he paying her a compliment or insulting her? "Suppose I don't want to go along?" she asked, playing devil's advocate. "You know, I've been thinking, too, and I've decided we don't get along well at all—or haven't you noticed that?"

He raised one eyebrow but said nothing.

She walked back into the living room. He followed. She turned to face him, intent on getting all of her thoughts out into the open. "We argue a lot. And we don't have much in common, when you think about it. You're just too... too intense for me."

"Intense? That's bad?" Before she could elaborate he'd taken a step closer, and then another. Even as he posed the seemingly sincere question, intensity spilled out of him. She could feel it in his coffee-brown eyes, in his unconsciously aggressive stance, in the way he invaded her personal space.

"Not bad, just..." What? *Exciting.* Now why had that word come to mind? When he looked as if he might come even closer in his impatience for her to explain, she unthinkingly reached out a hand to ward him off. She touched his arm, instantly aware that she'd made a mistake. The gentle contact brought him closer instead of nudging him away—so close that his warm breath ruffled her bangs.

He touched her chin with his finger and tipped her face up toward his. She closed her eyes and waited for the inevitable kiss. She'd been wanting this since the moment she had opened the door, she realized. But the contact never came. Suddenly he grabbed her shoulders in a painful grip, prompted by something other than passion. He jerked his head back, staring over her head in stunned amazement.

"What?" she asked, exasperated and suddenly aching for something that wasn't going to happen.

"Lindy, unless I'm hallucinating, there's a huge... snake... hanging from your light fixture."

She swiveled around to look, a sense of relief dulling her disappointment. "What are you doing up there?" she demanded of the snake.

She sounded neither scared nor particularly shocked, Thad noted as she pulled away from him. "I take it you're familiar with this creature?" he asked.

"A few minutes ago it was lying in that box, practically in a coma." As if it were no more than an old piece of rope, she disengaged the reptile from her chandelier. "Don't worry, it's harmless. It's a racer, a constrictor-type snake. Doesn't have much in the way of teeth. See?" She held the snake out for Thad's inspection as she let it harmlessly gum her index finger.

Thad took an involuntary step backward. "Is that your *pet?*" he asked, horrified.

She laughed and shook her head. "I rescued it this afternoon from my mother's cat. It was mauled pretty badly and seemed to be in a state of shock. I was planning to take it to work with me tomorrow, see if anything could be done—"

"You were going to take it to Kevin's insurance office?"

She laughed again, a sound Thad enjoyed more every time he heard it. "No, I'm not working there anymore. I started a new job this week at the nature center. We take in sick and injured animals, rehabilitate them, and then integrate them back into the wild. But Mr. Snake here—" she paused to stroke its length as it curled around her wrist "—seems to be recovering nicely on his own. Want to hold him?"

Thad held up his hand in a warding-off gesture. After coming so close to holding Lindy in his arms, the thought of cuddling a snake made his skin crawl. "No, thanks."

"Some risk-taker," Lindy murmured as she allowed the creature to coil around her neck.

The comment got to him. "All right, I'll hold the damn snake on one condition."

"What's that?"

"Go out with me."

She seemed to give his suggestion serious consideration. At least she hadn't said no right away, he thought. Then a mischievous light twinkled in her green eyes. "Okay," she finally said, just like that, as she unlooped the snake from her neck. She held it out to him. "Here."

He filed her affirmative answer in the back of his mind, to be dealt with later. Then he gingerly touched the snake,

surprised at how soft, dry and cool its skin was. He lightly
stroked it, and when it didn't seem to mind he let it slide over
the palm of his hand and wind around his arm. Suppress-
ing a shudder, he held it up so he could look into its little
black eyes. It gazed back at him blankly and flicked its
forked tongue.

Lindy smiled as she watched man and beast size each
other up. She couldn't believe she'd just agreed to go out
with him. Kevin had been right when he'd warned her of
Thad's serious nature. He didn't take anything casually—
even his approach to having fun was pretty no-nonsense.
She, on the other hand, took nothing seriously.

So it couldn't work out for Thad and her in the long run,
she decided with a frown. Not only were their life philoso-
phies diametrically opposed, but she simply did not have the
capacity for constancy. After all, she hadn't managed to
finish college or hold down the same job for more than a
few months. Her most enduring romantic liaison had self-
destructed after less than eight weeks. How could she expect to succeed in a lasting relationship?

Still, even knowing all that, she'd been powerless to turn
down Thad's invitation. His brick-wall facade was already
showing a few cracks, and she was intrigued by what she
might find underneath. There was also the fact that he was
one of the most potently sensual men she'd ever encoun-
tered. The temptation to be near him—to bathe in that raw
male sexuality—was too strong to resist.

"This isn't so bad," Thad finally said as the snake worked
its way up his arm. "I thought it would feel slimier."

"Haven't you ever held a snake before?" she asked.
"Even when you were a kid?"

He shook his head. "Weren't many snakes in the apartment buildings where I grew up. Hey, look at that," he said,
pointing to the small puncture wounds that marred the
snake's pattern of shiny scales. "Looks like the cat got in a
couple of good licks. Is it serious?"

"I don't think so. In fact, he's looking so chipper, I think we ought to let him go." Just then the snake made a dive for the neck of Thad's T-shirt. It was halfway down his chest before Lindy, hampered by Thad's squirming protests and her own clumsiness brought on by his nearness, could pull the slithering reptile free.

"That was not funny," Thad insisted, looking decidedly pale. "Holding a snake is one thing, having it inside my clothes is another."

Lindy struggled to hang on to her composure. The nervous giggle that threatened was due mostly to their brief but exciting physical contact. Then again, his aversion to the snake was pretty funny. She took a deep breath and managed to contain the laughter, deciding not to push her luck. She couldn't expect Thad to develop a sense of humor overnight.

"Shame on you," she admonished the snake, none too sternly. "It's definitely time to take you outside and turn you loose." And to Thad, she said, "Let's take him out to the trees behind the house. He'll have lots of dead leaves and things to hide under."

Thad nodded. He was more than ready to see the last of the creature.

It was an exceptionally dark, moonless evening, but even the faint starlight glinted in Lindy's spun-gold hair. Thad followed her down the stairs and through the backyard, aware of every inch of her taut body. He'd come very close to kissing her awhile ago, and with almost no provocation. He couldn't recall ever acting so impulsively with a woman. Just being near her caused his brain to short out and his hormones to take over.

"This looks good," she said, pausing amidst a small copse of trees. When Thad shrugged and nodded his agreement, she settled the snake on the ground. It raised its head, as if to get its bearings, then wasted no time in slithering away through the tall grass. "Stay away from cats," Lindy called softly.

They walked back to the garage in silence, pausing at the bottom of the stairs. "I held up my end of the bargain," he said, his voice faintly challenging. "How's Saturday night? The Saddle Club is having a rodeo."

"Are you sure you want to go out? The other day you insisted I would cause you nothing but trouble."

"You will," he said with utter certainty. "Seven o'clock?"

"Okay. But..."

"But what?"

She smiled and shook her head. "Nothing." She'd have to be straightforward with him. She'd have to let him know that she didn't intend to hang around Corrigan for long—just until her bout of homesickness went away. But not now, not yet. It was just one date, she told herself as she watched the rear reflector on his bike fade into the distance.

"So who are you going out with?" Marianne Shapiro asked Saturday afternoon as she stood in the doorway of her walk-in closet and allowed Lindy to rifle through her wardrobe. "Mmm, those beige pants would fit you."

Lindy examined the slacks thoughtfully. "Too tame."

"You're going to the rodeo, not on safari. I don't see why you don't just wear jeans like everybody else."

"My jeans all have holes in them."

"I thought holes were stylish."

"These holes are more like indecent—what's this?" Lindy asked, focusing her attention on a pink garment bag in the back of the closet.

"Oh, Lindy, you weren't supposed to see that. Now, don't unwrap—" But it was too late.

"It's perfect!" Lindy exclaimed, examining the white denim skirt and matching vest. Both pieces were trimmed in silver piping. But her sudden enthusiasm wilted as quickly as it had materialized as she turned a worried look toward Marianne. "It's brand-new, isn't it? You haven't even worn it yet." She sighed. "That's okay, I'll find something else."

"No, don't bother," said Marianne, retreating from the closet to stand in front of her dresser. She absently smoothed her silver-gilded blond hair away from her face. "It's yours. I found it at the mall in Nacogdoches. I was planning to give it to you for your birthday."

"Really?" Lindy took a closer look at the outfit. She and her mother might have their differences, but she couldn't argue with Marianne's taste in clothes. Even when she was just puttering around the house, she wore coordinated outfits. Today she had on a slimming pair of gray jeans and a pink-and-gray-striped golf shirt. "You're not just saying that to be nice?"

"Take a look at that hemline, sweetheart. I haven't worn a skirt that short in twenty years."

Lindy brought the outfit out of the closet and held it up to her body, examining her image in the full-length mirror. A smile spread slowly across her face. "It's perfect," she said again. "But I guess I really should wait for my birthday. It's not till next month."

"Nonsense. You might as well wear it now. Happy birthday, a few weeks early." She walked over and gave Lindy's shoulders a squeeze. "So who's the lucky stud? It's been a long time since I've seen you in a dither over clothes."

Lindy peeled off her old jeans so she could try on the denim outfit. "Sheriff Halsey," she announced casually, as she yanked the last leg of her tight pants off. When she looked to see her mother's reaction, Marianne was frowning. "What's wrong?" Lindy asked. "I thought you'd be pleased that I'm going out with a fine, upstanding citizen for a change."

That made Marianne smile. "I'm sorry, honey. I am pleased. I like Thad a great deal. It's just that...well, nothing."

Lindy sank onto her mother's king-size bed, the new clothes momentarily forgotten. "I'm not nice enough for him, is that it? That's what Kevin said, more or less."

"Oh, Kevin's fallen off horses and onto his head too many times," Marianne replied, dismissing her son with a wave of her hand. "That's not it. But Thad is awfully..."

"Intense? Serious? Solemn? Stodgy?" Lindy supplied. All of those words, and lots of others, had been chasing themselves around in her head ever since Thursday night.

"Exactly."

"Actually that's why he wants to go out with me. He wants to lighten up, and I'm going to help him." She pulled the short skirt off its hanger and stepped into it. It fit perfectly, molding to her derriere with the hem hitting well above her knees.

"Here, try this with it," Marianne said, handing Lindy a red cotton blouse. "He's never dated anyone from around here, you know."

Lindy pulled off her T-shirt and then paused. "Really?"

"Every available woman in the county and several unavailable ones have tried, too. You must have made quite an impression."

"I did that, all right." She cast aside her T-shirt and tried the red blouse on. "What do you think? Collar up or down?"

"Down. You won't break his heart, will you?"

"Aren't you worried he'll break mine?" Lindy asked, raising one eyebrow.

"You? A broken heart? That'll be the day. You're always the one who gets bored and walks off."

Lindy smiled wistfully. "I know. You told me once that I changed boyfriends as often as I changed clothes."

"In high school you just about did."

"I still do," she admitted. "Think I'll ever grow out of it?" she asked, suddenly serious. "Do you think I'll ever fall in love, get married and have kids like a normal person?"

"When you're ready," Marianne replied with a laugh. "One of these days, the nesting instinct will catch up with you—but I'm not holding my breath. Meanwhile . . . just be careful with Thad. Something tells me that behind that tough-guy exterior he's easily hurt. He's had a rough life."

"Everyone keeps saying that," Lindy said impatiently. "No one has an easy life. I grew up without a father, you've been without a husband for fifteen years—"

"Thad never even knew who his father was, and his mother didn't want him."

Lindy felt her face redden. "I'm sorry. I forget, sometimes, how lucky I've been. And don't worry about Thad, or me. I plan to keep it light." She laughed suddenly. "Gawd, we just met and you've already got us traumatically estranged."

The rodeo was a small one, but nonetheless it was surrounded by a rowdy atmosphere. Many of the competitors were high school kids, honing their skills for bigger contests in their futures. Hopes were high, and the kids' nerves were as taut as those of any competitor on the national circuit.

Thad shared that expectancy as he sat next to Lindy on the gray, splintered bleachers—close, but not touching. His nerves were attuned to something quite different than roping and riding, however. Though he enjoyed her company in any form, his mind kept wandering to the moment when he would have her to himself, when he could kiss her long, graceful neck and run his fingers through her incredibly bright, soft hair.

Now he struggled not to touch her. He was already the object of quite a bit of covert attention. Because he truly enjoyed all the trappings of small-town life, he was a frequent spectator at these homespun events. But he seldom showed up at one with a woman in tow. The whispers and the hooded glances were impossible to miss.

Lindy elicited plenty of attention on her own merit. The white skirt and vest enhanced her bronze skin and showed just enough of her slim legs to cause the men to look twice. He'd looked more than twice, haunted by the image of what might be hidden beneath the denim.

She smiled and called out a greeting to virtually every person who passed within her vision. Everyone knew her—she seemed to be universally adored by young and old, male and female.

"This is fun," Lindy commented during a lull in the calf-roping competition. "I haven't been to one of these rodeos in years. I used to barrel race when I was a kid. Kevin and I both used to compete in these things in high school. He stayed with it, though. He's pretty good."

"He is," Thad agreed. "I've seen him ride. In fact, a couple of months ago—" He broke off midsentence as his attention was drawn to something behind Lindy. He waved to someone she couldn't see. By the time Lindy turned around, he was gesturing for a dark-haired woman to join them.

Twyla Jessup. Of all the people in the county, why did he have to know *her?* She'd alternately been Lindy's best friend and arch enemy all through high school. They had competed for everything—head cheerleader, homecoming queen, class president. Twyla also had had an annoying habit of aggressively pursuing any boy who showed an interest in Lindy.

Thad stood as the petite, dark-haired Twyla approached. "Hi, Thad." She smiled, revealing her perfectly straight teeth. Then her eyes fell on Lindy, and the smile broadened. "Lindy! I'd heard you were back. Why didn't you call me?"

"I thought you were still living in Tyler," Lindy said as she stood to return the hug offered by her old friend and nemesis, feeling a wave of nostalgia. They'd had some pretty good cat fights in their day, but when they got along they did so splendidly. They were too much alike, Lindy's mother had always said. Or at least, they used to be. After high school Twyla had married and started a family.

"I moved back home when Billy and I split up a couple of years ago," Twyla said.

Oh, terrific. Twyla was single, and no doubt looking. Lindy felt an immediate surge of possessiveness toward Thad. When she sat back down, she settled a little closer to him, so that their thighs brushed. With the light physical contact came a sudden rush of heat, which only fueled her primitive urge to stake a claim on the sexiest male in Scanlon County.

"I didn't mean to be so late," Twyla said as she sat down on the bleacher above them, so she could lean down and talk to them both. "We didn't miss the saddle broncs, did we? The bucking broncos are Jeffrey's favorite."

Jeffrey? Lindy wondered.

"How's he doing these days?" Thad asked, making Lindy feel left out. Obviously he knew who Jeffrey was.

"Jeffrey's my son," Twyla said for Lindy's benefit. "And he's doing better. Much better. He'll be here in a minute and you can see for yourself. He stopped to get popcorn." She laid a hand on Thad's shoulder. "He really likes you, Thad. You've been a good role model for him. We both know Billy wasn't much of an example."

Lindy bristled at the implied intimacy between her erstwhile friend and her date. If Twyla was sporting for a battle, she'd get one.

"You staying for the dance later?" Thad asked casually.

"I guess I will, if Mom and Dad will take Jeffrey."

Lindy maintained a serene expression while inwardly she seethed. Thad was with *her.* How dare he flirt with Twyla?

"We're staying, aren't we, Lindy?" Thad asked.

"I do have to work tomorrow," she reminded him coolly.

Twyla laughed. "Oh, Lindy, since when did you let a job stop you from having a good time? Why don't y'all stay? At least for a while."

Lindy made a noncommittal reply. At least Twyla hadn't suggested that Thad stay and Lindy go home to bed. At one time, she wouldn't have hesitated.

As the bulldogging got under way, a four-foot dynamo barreled up the bleachers toward them, a half-empty bag of popcorn clutched in one tight fist. "Hi, Sheriff!" the little boy called out with a snaggle-toothed grin. When he was close enough, he extended his other hand for a grown-up greeting, which Thad obliged.

"That's quite a grip," said Thad. "Say, how did you like camp?"

"It was neat," Jeffrey said. "I got to ride horses and cook with a fire and sleep outside and everything."

"Thanks again, Thad," Twyla said, "for arranging things so Jeffrey could go." She turned to Lindy. "I don't think you've ever met my son."

"No, I haven't," Lindy replied, charmed by the freckle-faced boy despite herself. "Hi, Jeffrey. I'm Lindy."

"Nice to meet you," he mumbled shyly.

"You call her 'Miss Shapiro,'" Twyla insisted in a stern, motherly tone that made Lindy smile secretly.

They all turned their attention to the events taking place in the arena, but Thad and Jeffrey carried on an animated conversation the whole time. The camaraderie between the two gave Lindy a peculiar ache in the pit of her stomach. She'd never thought much about children, always assuming that someday in the distant future she would have them. Now, suddenly, she found herself wishing that she had a little boy like Jeffrey.

Twyla took such pride in him, and she was obviously doing a good job raising him. She wasn't the same flighty, irresponsible girl she had been in high school. She'd changed.

And I haven't.

She shook her head to clear it of errant thoughts. It was just a dose of good, old-fashioned jealousy that made her think such weird things. She'd always been jealous of Twyla—her petite stature, her full breasts, her huge, almond-shaped brown eyes. But that was when they were just girls, Lindy reminded herself.

"Look, Mom, they're about to start the bronc riding. Can I go up closer?"

Twyla nodded to her son. "All right. Let's both go see if we can find a place by the fence." She gave Thad and Lindy an apologetic smile. "Keep your fingers crossed."

"What did she mean by that?" Lindy asked when Twyla was out of earshot.

Thad gave her a look of amusement. "You don't know?"

She pursed her lips. "The only thing I know is that you're on pretty warm terms with her. It's bad form, you know, to ask a woman to a dance when you're already with another one." She sounded petulant; she knew it, and still couldn't stop herself.

"Why, Lindy Shapiro, you're jealous."

"I am not!" she denied hotly. "It's just that I know how Twyla operates...." She sounded like a whiny adolescent, she realized miserably. Why had she ever started this stupid argument?

"Kevin said you and Twyla used to be best friends."

"We were. And what does Kevin have to do with this?"

Thad chuckled. "You really don't know."

"Know what?" Lindy demanded.

"Twyla isn't the slightest bit interested in me. Someone else has her eye, but he's busy at the moment riding the broncs."

"*Kevin?* Twyla and *Kevin?*" So that's what she'd meant when she had told them to keep their fingers crossed. She was wishing Kevin good luck. "He couldn't stand her when we were in high school."

Thad rolled his eyes. "A lot you know. Anyway, Kevin asked me if I'd keep an eye out for Twyla and Jeffrey, and make sure they were enjoying themselves and that they had someone to talk to."

"Since when does Twyla need an assist in that department?" Lindy asked skeptically. "She can always find someone to talk to, usually the nearest good-looking male."

Thad's expression grew serious. "I didn't know her before, but she's not like that now."

"How do you know her so well?" Lindy asked, careful not to make it an accusation. She'd already embarrassed herself with her childish behavior.

"Her ex-husband caused her some problems when she first moved back to Corrigan, about the same time I moved down here. I got called in for a domestic disturbance—several, as a matter of fact. She and Jeffrey needed help getting rid of the guy. I helped her," he said simply.

Lindy chose her words carefully. She hated herself for even asking, but she had to know. "Were you . . . involved with her?"

"Would you care?"

"Yes." She wasn't sure she could live with the knowledge that her old friend had been to bed with Thad—not when she intended to deny herself the same pleasure.

He gave her a lazy smile—one of the few she'd seen. "No, Twyla and I have never been intimate." He slipped his arm around Lindy and pulled her closer. "You're cute when you're jealous."

Five

___

Keep it light. Keep it light. Lindy chanted this refrain to herself incessantly during the remainder of the rodeo, and at the outdoor dance later. Kevin had warned her not to trifle with Thad's feelings. Her mother had begged her not to break his heart. Thad himself had predicted she'd bring trouble into his life, and she would do all three unless she was damn careful.

She was afraid that if Thad decided to feel something, he'd feel it deeply. If those feelings were focused on her, she would never be able to retreat gracefully.

Then again, why was she so worried about his feelings, when she was the one who hyperventilated every time he came within touching distance?

Her only hope was to keep their relationship light and fun. They would share a few dates, she'd loosen him up a little, and then she'd be on her way.

Miami. That was her next destination, as soon as summer was over. She had a friend who could get her a job as a maid on a cruise ship.

She tried to focus on the thought of bright blue water and palm trees swaying in the warm trade winds as she and Thad slow-danced to an old Hank Williams song. But as her feet moved noiselessly through the grass, her heart felt like a bird beating its wings against a cage, and every inch of her skin flamed with awareness.

He held her much too close, but she couldn't make herself do anything about it. Even in the eighty-five-degree heat, she savored the warmth of his body. She found herself pressing her cheek against his crisp cotton shirt, trying to catch a whiff of his clean, subtle scent. His hand was hot against her back where he'd slipped it under her vest. She wondered how it would feel against bare skin.

Her own hand glided from his shoulder to the back of his neck, unable to resist the urge to feel the thick, golden-brown hair that curled there in the summer humidity. It was softer than she thought it would be, and she felt a ridiculous urge to bury her face in it.

When his lips brushed her neck, almost as if by accident, Lindy knew she was in trouble. Willpower was not high on her list of strengths, and she couldn't depend on Thad to keep his distance. With all her talk about taking risks and having fun, she'd practically given him an engraved invitation.

Even when the song ended, they didn't pull apart. Instead, Thad wrapped both arms around her, pressing her so tightly against him that the air whooshed out of her lungs.

"Shouldn't we be clapping for the band?" she asked, purposely wedging the real world between them.

"What for?" he said, his voice rough. "They're worse than Pete and the Pit Bulls." But he did release her.

She laughed as an unexpected breeze wafted through the crowd of dancers, vibrating the canopy overhead and cooling her flushed skin. "You really don't like country music, do you?"

"Not really."

"But how did you learn to dance? I've never danced with anyone who made it so effortless."

"That's not me. That's us. We're good together."

His words gave her a delicious shiver. Instinctively she knew they'd be good at other activities, too. Suddenly she was impatient to conclude the evening. The suspense was twisting her stomach into knots. "Are you ready to go?"

He nodded, and she was afraid he understood her impatience all too well.

They said a quick goodbye to Twyla and Kevin. Lindy had been watching them covertly, still finding it hard to believe that the two of them could even like each other. They'd danced together to almost every song, smiling and talking, but they'd maintained a healthy distance.

She couldn't remember Twyla ever being so cautious where a male of the species was concerned. In high school, if she was at all attracted, she would go after the poor, unsuspecting guy with the full force of her charms. If she wasn't interested, she wouldn't waste her time.

"Have they been going out long?" Lindy asked Thad as they left the tent and headed toward the parking lot. They held hands, so that even as they carried on a normal conversation, she could not escape the memory of his touch and the fire it ignited.

"Kevin and Twyla? A few weeks, I think."

"That long?"

"You're really surprised, aren't you?"

She shrugged. "It's just that Twyla doesn't act the way I remember her. But then it's been a lot of years."

"A lot of years that weren't very good to her. That ex-husband of hers . . ." He shook his head in obvious disgust. "And Jeffrey—it's a real relief to see him acting like a normal kid. When I first met him, I couldn't get him to crack a smile for anything.''

''Kinda like you,'' Lindy commented lazily. They'd reached Thad's truck, but instead of getting inside, she leaned back against the hood, propped on her elbows. ''I still can't get you to smile.''

He stood in front of her, leaned forward and placed his hands on the truck on either side of her. ''I bet you could if you tried.''

Her mind quickly sifted through all the ways she could try, but she settled on the safest one. She reached out and tickled him.

''Oh, no you don't!'' He grabbed her wrists and pulled her hands a safe distance from his midsection. ''That's definitely not what I had in mind.''

''Oh, yeah?'' But there was little defiance to her breathless protest.

He could have kissed her then, and the need to have his arms around her again was almost overwhelming. But he still had enough presence of mind to remember they were in the fairgrounds parking lot. Slowly he released her, knowing she wouldn't try to tickle him again.

He started to open her door when she let out a squeal and jumped as if she'd been scalded.

''What is it?'' Every muscle in his body tensed, ready to do battle with the unknown enemy. But Lindy, recovering quickly, was already bending over to examine whatever had startled her—a burlap bag lying in the grass by the truck's front tire.

''It's a dog,'' she said as she opened the bag. ''A puppy.''

Thad opened the truck door. The dome light illuminated a tiny black-and-tan bundle of fur.

''Thank goodness he wiggled against my foot,'' she said, ''or we might have driven right over him.'' Without hesitation she scooped the pup into her hands and held him up to the light. ''This puppy's barely weaned.'' She looked suddenly fierce even as she cuddled the animal against her breast. "Who could abandon something this sweet and helpless?"

The dog whimpered and squirmed, then nestled in the crook of her arm.

"What are you going to do with it?" Thad asked. He resented the puppy's intrusion, then felt like a heel for doing so.

"I don't know. But we can't just leave it here, it'll die."

First it was sparrows, then a snake, and now a dog, he thought as he tentatively touched one finger to the puppy's soft fur. Next time he and Lindy were together, he couldn't imagine what they might rescue. An elephant?

So much for any romantic notions he might have had, he mused as he helped her into the truck cab. The sensual aura that had surrounded them at the dance like a warm blanket was rapidly disintegrating. He couldn't compete with small, furry creatures—hell, even a scaly snake had been enough to distract her from him.

After he'd started the engine he glanced over at her. She looked warm and maternal, stroking the animal with her long, graceful hands, and his momentary irritation vanished. He didn't want or expect her to behave any other way. Part of what made Lindy so appealing was her compassion.

It was probably just as well, he thought, trying to console himself. He'd been about to rush things, anyway.

"Are you going to keep it?" he asked.

"No," she answered without hesitation. "I...I can't have a dog, not while I'm living in that apartment. Mother's cat goes bonkers. And anyway, I don't allow myself to keep pets. I move around too much. In fact..." She took a deep breath. "I'll be leaving at the end of the summer."

"Oh? Where are you going?" he asked, feeling like he'd been punched in the stomach. He'd known she probably wouldn't stay in Corrigan indefinitely—she'd already told him as much. Why did putting a date to her departure knock the wind out of him?

"Miami," she answered. "I've always wanted to work on a cruise ship, and I have a friend who can get me a job on the *Bahama Queen.*"

"Sounds . . . different. What will you do with him?" He nodded toward the puppy.

"Why don't you take him?" she suggested.

"Me?" He shook his head vehemently. "No way. I don't know anything about dogs."

"You mean you never had a dog?" she asked, her voice all soft and velvety.

"No, not unless you count the stray that tried to adopt me in high school. My mother wouldn't let me keep it." She'd made him take the dog far away from their apartment building and lose it, he remembered, but he decided not to tell Lindy that part.

"Then you've missed a very important lesson in life," she replied pragmatically. "Everyone needs to know what it's like to be responsible for another living thing."

"Why do I get the feeling I'm being set up?"

"Just take him home for the night," Lindy said, resorting to a direct approach. "Give him some water and some food, then put him in a box with a blanket and a hot water bottle and a ticking clock, and you won't have any problems. I'll find him a home tomorrow."

"If it's just for one night, you take him," Thad argued sensibly.

"I have to work tomorrow. You have the day off," she countered.

He sighed. "All right, I'll take the puppy home. For one night. On one condition."

"Yes, I'd like to see you again," she said, smiling in the darkness.

Damn. How had she known that's what he was going to ask? "I'm entirely too predictable," he said. "I'll have to work on that."

"Thad," she said after a short silence, "what was it like for you, growing up?"

He gritted his teeth in an automatic reaction, then forced himself to relax his jaw. "You must already know, or you wouldn't ask."

"I don't know much, and I don't mean to pry, but—"

"I don't make a secret of my past," he cut in. "I grew up poor, and my mom pretty much ignored me, but that just taught me to be resourceful."

"Seems you did all right for yourself," she added, sensing the subtle shade of resentfulness that tainted his childhood memories.

"Yeah."

She could have kicked herself for bringing up the subject in the first place. She'd wanted to bring them closer, and instead she had planted a brick wall firmly between them again.

By the time Thad turned into her driveway, they'd begun to talk about less sensitive subjects, but their earlier good humor had been irreparably dampened. He parked his truck behind her car and they both got out, but he paused at the stairs.

"I'm stopping here," he said. If he didn't, if he went all the way inside her apartment, he might not want to leave. He leaned forward and kissed her lightly on the cheek, then the mouth. Her response was instantaneous and, he was certain, completely uncalculated. Her mouth was warm and welcoming, full of promise and seeming to hold the very mysteries of life. Though he hadn't intended to, he grasped her shoulders and pulled her against him, gently plumbing her depths with his tongue.

God, she was sweet. And he was painfully aroused.

The puppy squirmed in protest at being squashed between them. Abruptly Lindy broke off the kiss and thrust the warm, furry bundle at Thad. "Don't forget Freddy," she said, breathing hard.

Startled, he accepted the animal as he tried to get his brainwaves back in order. Damn, but Lindy Shapiro did something powerful to him. Somehow he managed a coherent rejoinder. "Freddy?"

"Reminds me of my Great-Uncle Fred," she explained with a shrug.

"That's a terrible name for a dog."

She giggled nervously. "Especially since it's a female. You name her."

He held on to the puppy awkwardly. "A name, huh? I'll have to think about it. Are you sure I should take her? What if I—"

"You'll do fine. Good night, Thad."

He nodded, accepting her dismissal for what it was—a self-protective gesture. She was every bit as off balance as he was, which gave him some comfort. He got into his truck, settled "Freddy" onto his lap and started the engine.

Lindy watched him go, her body pulsing from that one, brief contact of his mouth to hers. Her physical reaction to him was as hot and unpredictable as wildfire. If the kiss had lasted another thirty seconds, no telling what would have happened.

She felt incomplete, suddenly aching to feel his mouth hard against hers once more, to feel his chest rise and fall as they breathed in unison. Part of her deeply regretted sending him away. But another part of her was undeniably relieved. She didn't want to see her relationship with Thad follow the usual pattern. She didn't want to see it bloom in a burst of passion, then self-destruct, and that's exactly what would happen if they became intimate.

No, it was much better if they didn't. The puppy had made a handy distraction tonight, but what about next time?

Keep it light, she chanted as she slowly made her way up the creaky stairs.

Work at the Scanlon County Junior College Nature Center began well before its doors opened to the public. There were cages to be cleaned, food and water to be replenished, medication to be given and bandages to be changed. Lindy, the first to arrive on that Sunday morning, went after the first two tasks with a surplus of energy. She loved being around the wild animals.

The last two tasks—medication and bandages—would have to wait until Dr. Wang arrived. Lindy had only been working there a week and was reluctant to administer any sort of medical care without the veterinarian to supervise.

A red-tailed hawk with a broken wing eyed her suspiciously as she changed the newspaper in his cage. Although he was obviously frightened of her, she kept a wary eye on him, having been warned that his talons were lethal. "You're looking chipper this morning," she said to the bird. Testing, she held a gloved finger close to its beak. It let out a piercing shriek and attacked.

She quickly withdrew her hand and closed the cage door.

"Good morning, Lindy," came a cheery greeting from the direction of the front door. Lindy turned to see Dr. Dorothy Wang's diminutive form bustling toward her, travel mug full of steaming coffee in one hand and a notebook in the other. She wore faded jeans and a tank shirt, and her coal-black hair was pulled back in a careless ponytail.

"Hey, Dottie," Lindy called back. "Everybody looks good this morning. Even Hubert the Hawk is showing his temper."

Dottie frowned in mock disapproval. "I told you to stop naming the animals. You name them, you get attached to them, then you don't want to let them go."

"I get attached to them, anyway. Maybe that's why..." She didn't finish the sentence.

"Maybe that's why what?" Dottie asked, narrowing her eyes speculatively.

"Oh, nothing, really. I was going to say maybe that's why I didn't become a vet—I get too attached to animals and I hate to see them suffer. But that's not the reason."

"Oh? What is the reason?" Dottie asked, unduly interested.

"I couldn't hack the classes," Lindy replied carelessly.

"Did you try?"

"I was in prevet for about half a semester, but that was just the first in a long string of majors—sociology, broadcast journalism, medieval history..." She shrugged. "That was a long time ago."

Dottie looked as if she might pursue the subject, but then seemed to change her mind. Instead, she focused her attention on the hawk. "So, Hubert, we're ornery today? That's a good sign."

With Dottie's sharp black eyes keeping watch, Lindy administered pills and syringes full of medicine to various and sundry injured and ill raccoons, rabbits, opossums, skunks, birds and even an armadillo. The two women were in the process of rebandaging the foot of an adolescent beaver, which had gotten caught in some fishing line, when the phone rang.

"I'll get it," Lindy said as she stood and walked toward the phone on the wall. "Nature center."

"If you don't get over here in the next thirty minutes and fetch this puppy from hell, I'm going to drown it."

"Thad?"

"Yes, Thad! Who did you think?"

The irritable, sarcastic brute on the other end of the phone was not the sensible, even-tempered man she'd been with last night. Freddy must have indeed exceeded her welcome.

"Just sit tight," she said patiently. "I'll be there as soon as I can. Where exactly do you live, anyway?"

He gave her terse directions.

"Um, Dottie?" Lindy said when she'd hung up.

"I heard," the older woman said, unconsciously stroking the beaver. "Sounds like an emergency."

"Sort of. A puppy's life may be at stake," Lindy explained. "Can I... bring it here? I know we're not supposed to take in domestic animals, but it's so tiny and someone dumped it at the fairgrounds and—"

"All right, all right. You can bring it here. But find it a home—fast. Go on," she urged when Lindy came to help her finish up the beaver. "I've got Belinda here under control."

Lindy rushed toward the small office to retrieve her purse, but she slowed down long enough to flash a grateful smile in Dottie's direction. In the short time she'd been working with Dottie Wang, she'd grown to like and respect her a lot. "I'll be forty-five minutes—an hour, tops."

"Take as long as you need. We don't have any classes today, and with this heat we aren't likely to have much walk-in traffic."

Lindy had no trouble finding the beige brick house in Star Harbor. It looked like the sort of home Thad Halsey would have—neat, no-nonsense, with a well-trimmed yard and an often-swept front porch. She punched the doorbell with a decisive jab, ready to give Thad a piece of her mind. Anyone who would even *think* of drowning a puppy ought to be put away.

No one answered. She rang again, but all was still.

He had to be home. She tried the door, and when it gave, she opened it a crack and peeked inside. "Thad?"

Still nothing.

Cautiously she made her way through a small, tiled entry hall that led into the living room—and froze. In the middle of the room sat a nubby white sofa, and sprawled across it was Thad—sleeping soundly. His bare feet hung over one arm of the couch. He wore nothing but a pair of navy-blue sweatpants that delineated every gorgeous muscle in his legs to perfection. The thin cotton stretched invitingly across his pelvis, leaving little to Lindy's imagination.

Her face grew warm even as she continued to stare, sure she could never drink in her fill of the sight of him. One tanned forearm was thrown across his face, blocking the light from his eyes. The other rested gently atop the black-and-tan puppy that was curled up in the middle of his bare chest, snoring blissfully.

Shaking herself out of her lustful trance, Lindy forced herself to examine the rest of the room, which told an eloquent story. In one corner a cardboard box lay on its side, its contents spilled onto the floor. The rest of the room was utter chaos—a trail of shredded books, magazines and shoes; houseplants overturned, their once-lush green leaves hopelessly mangled; several little indiscretions marring the celery-green carpet.

Lindy's stomach sank at the implications. She'd hoped the puppy might find a permanent home here, but now that seemed highly unlikely.

"Oh, Freddy, how could you?" she murmured, resisting the urge to awaken the pooch and throttle her. No wonder Thad had threatened to drown her. The place looked like Sherman's army had marched through.

Lindy decided to take advantage of the momentary quiet and try to minimize the damage. She was an old pro at disguising the disasters wrought by her various pets over the years. She uprighted the plants and scooped the dirt back into them. Anything that was chewed beyond recognition she threw away, and the rest she reshelved.

She found Thad's leather wallet hiding under a chair, pocked with tooth marks. Its contents had spilled out. She had to smile at the stern photo on his driver's license before tucking it back inside and setting the wallet on the coffee table.

Some soap and water took care of the housebreaking errors. By the time she was finished, the place didn't look half bad.

She had just started a pot of coffee in the cheerful red-and-white kitchen when she heard her name. Startled, she turned to find Thad standing in the doorway, looking touchably rumpled and adorably confused. The now-docile puppy was draped limply over his arm.

"What are you doing here?" he asked in a scratchy voice.

"You called for reinforcements, remember?"

He closed his eyes for a moment. "Oh, yeah. Guess I fell asleep. The devil-pup cried all night, didn't stop until about five this morning—that must have been when she escaped from the box and redecorated my living room. I take it she didn't clean it up, so you must have. Thanks."

Lindy looked down at the toes of her tennis shoes. "I shouldn't have pushed you to take her," she said. "I hope she didn't damage anything really valuable."

Thad shrugged. "I don't own anything really valuable."

"Well," Lindy said with forced briskness, "I can keep Freddy at the nature center till I find her a home." She reached to take the puppy from Thad.

He surprised her by resisting. "Wait a minute. You want to take her away?"

"That's what you asked me to do, isn't it?"

"Yeah, but..." The puppy looked up at him with adoring eyes and wagged her fat little tail.

He wasn't a quitter, dammit. He refused to let a pint-sized mongrel defeat him. He would teach this hellhound some manners if it killed him. "I'll mind her just until you find her a permanent home," he said.

"Can I trust you not to pitch her into the lake?"

He winced as he recalled how sharply he'd spoken to Lindy over the phone. "I would never hurt her," he said, holding the puppy just a little more tightly. "I get a little grouchy when I'm deprived of sleep, that's all."

Lindy looked as if she wanted to agree with him. "Are you sure?"

He nodded.

"She needs housebreaking. I'd stay and help, but I really have to get back to work."

"Sorry I dragged you all the way out here," he said, though he couldn't deny he enjoyed seeing her again. He'd thought about her all last night. If Freddy's piercing yips and whines hadn't kept him awake, thoughts of Lindy would have. He tried to think of something to say that would make her want to stay awhile, but came up blank.

"I'll forgive you—this time." She gave the puppy a parting pat, which was more of a goodbye than Thad got.

He stood at the front door, breathing deeply of the fresh scent she'd left behind, and watched her swing her jeans-clad legs into the Cadillac.

Housebreaking? he thought, a little bewildered. How was he supposed to do that? He took the pup outside and set her down in the grass. She sniffed at leaves and bugs for several unproductive minutes.

Thad wasn't sure what exactly had possessed him to keep the mutt, but he suspected it had something to do with the vaguely disappointed look in Lindy's bright green eyes when he'd first faced her in the kitchen, and the faint coolness in her voice. He had let her down. He hated to let anyone down.

The puppy cornered a grasshopper and growled at it. Thad laughed. "Oh, you're fierce, aren't you, Freddy?" He scooped her up and rubbed her soft fur against his unshaven cheek, then touched her cold, wet nose to his. She

licked his face in what he took to be a blatant apology for all
the havoc she'd wreaked on his life.

Something tightened inside his chest and his eyes stung.
He stared up at the cloudless blue sky until the strange feeling passed.

Thad watched in silent amazement as about four dozen
teenagers wielded paintbrushes and rollers, lawn mowers,
and hammers and nails, miraculously transforming Hazel
Ecklund's tired farm into a showplace.

He had to hand it to Lindy. She had the organizational
skills of a military tactical expert. She'd taken two problems—rampant juvenile delinquency and Hazel's financial
straits—and combined them into a summer youth project.
Kids who volunteered a day of community service were re-
warded with a party at the VFW hall. Lindy had elicited the
cooperation of a paint company, a soft drink distributor and
a deejay who would spin dance tunes at the party.

If the initial project worked out—and it showed all signs
of being an unqualified success—she intended to expand the
program to fill the remaining weeks of summer.

She was one heck of an organizer, all right, but where was
she when it was time to do the *real* work? Thad grumbled to
himself. Not only was today his day off, but it was also his
birthday, and he was spending it toiling in the hot sun, su-
pervising the painting and repairs. Alone.

It was just like her to get this thing all organized and then
dump it in his lap, he mused, shaking his head. He was
coming to realize that she was pretty good at starting things,
but not very good at completing them. Unfortunately he
himself would probably be included among her list of unfinished projects. At the end of August, she still planned to
take off for Miami, and Thad was helpless to stop her.

Just a month left. That wasn't nearly enough time to explore the complicated, confusing relationship that was
growing between them. He was at once challenged and

frustrated by the puzzle she represented, excited and downright frightened by the alien feelings she awakened in him.

One of those feelings, at least, he understood—acute lust. He felt it every time he so much as thought about her lean, taut body and her smooth, golden skin. Even her ready smile could cause his stomach to tighten. Her scent, as fresh and invigorating as the promise of spring, set his very blood on fire.

She felt it, too. He could see it simmering just under the surface, precariously banked behind her intense green gaze. Yet as mutual as their attraction was, he'd never managed more than a few desperately stolen kisses with her. They'd been together several times since the rodeo, but each of their dates had been carefully orchestrated by Lindy so that they were never completely alone.

Her behavior puzzled him. For someone who grabbed on to life with as much fervor as she did, she was exhibiting uncharacteristic caution where physical intimacy was concerned.

"Hey, where's Lindy?" a towheaded fifteen-year-old girl asked Thad. It wasn't the first time today he'd been asked that question.

All he could do was shrug. "I'm not sure. She might be setting up for the party. That's a nice job you're doing on the fence," he said, even though the girl had been paying more attention to the sixteen-year-old boy painting the other side of the fence than she had on her own work.

Still, she beamed in response. "Thanks. I never painted anything before—not with a brush, anyway. It's kinda fun."

He imagined she'd feel more at ease with a can of spray paint, but he kept that thought to himself.

Shortly after lunch, Jimmy McGruder showed up to relieve Thad. "Any words of wisdom before you go?" the young deputy asked, surveying the energetic teenagers with trepidation.

"Just keep on the lookout for paint fights and put a stop to them as quickly as you can. And don't let any precocious couples wander into the hayloft."

Jimmy nodded. "Oh, I almost forgot. Belva wants you to stop by the office before you go home. She needs your signature on something."

Thad made an impatient sound at the back of his throat. He was dying to get home, shuck his sweaty clothes and go for a swim in the lake. He was scheduled to chaperon the party this evening, and he wanted to take advantage of the little free time he had left. "Can't it wait till Monday?"

Jimmy shook his head. "She said she has to get it in the mail today."

The office was hardly on his way home, but Thad supposed he'd have to postpone his swim a few minutes longer. "If Lindy ever shows up," he said over his shoulder as he made his way to his truck, "tell her...oh, never mind. I'll see her later." He wasn't sure what he wanted to tell her, he thought as he drove toward the sheriff's office in Winstonia. He was undeniably irritated that she'd left him alone and defenseless against an unruly bunch of juvenile delinquents armed with paint, but he knew he didn't have the right to be too angry, not when she'd organized the whole project single-handedly.

He waltzed through the front doors of the county courthouse, around the corner, and into the sheriff's office, his mind already focusing on the refreshing dip in the lake he had planned. Maybe he'd take Freddy with him. Surely with those big, paddlelike feet of hers she could learn to swim.

He'd taken two steps across the waiting area when a resounding "Surprise!" broke through his musings. It was then that he saw the ceiling full of helium balloons and walls dripping with purple-and-yellow crepe paper. Behind Belva's desk, where they'd apparently been hiding, stood a small group of people who could be loosely described as his closest friends—deputy Chet Klingstedt and his wife, Eloise;

Kevin, Twyla and Jeffrey; and the ever-cheerful Belva. Also present was Les, the elderly county maintenance technician who had no doubt wandered through the office at an opportune moment.

In the center of the group was Lindy, looking sassy and sexy in another of her miniskirts—pink, this time—and grinning ear-to-ear, obviously pleased with herself.

Thad was stunned to the bone. A surprise party. No one had ever done such a thing for him before. He was touched by Lindy's thoughtfulness—and irritated that he would have to endure his one and only birthday party in such a sweaty, paint-spattered state, especially when she was primrose-fresh.

"Don't just stand there, make a speech or something," Chet said.

Thad finally managed an uneasy smile. "I'm floored. How did you know it was my birthday?"

"I sneaked a peek at your driver's license when I was cleaning up after Freddy," Lindy answered as she popped the cork on a bottle of champagne.

A brightly iced sheet cake appeared from somewhere, complete with candles. The group sang an off-key version of "Happy Birthday," much to Thad's acute embarrassment, and forced him to blow out the candles and cut the cake.

"What'd you wish for?" Jeffrey piped up.

Thad gave Lindy a meaningful look that made her blush and turn away, suddenly absorbed with licking icing off the end of her finger. "World peace," he said, though at that moment he would have been quite satisfied with a little inner peace.

When Twyla handed him a glass of champagne, his well-honed sense of duty reasserted itself. "We aren't supposed to have alcohol in a government building," he reminded everyone. At least Chet, still officially on duty, didn't partake.

"Now, Thad, don't be a party pooper," said Lindy in her most persuasive voice. She placed a gaudy, pointed cardboard hat on his head, snapping the elastic under his chin. "We'll just have one teeny drink and then clear out so Belva and Chet can get back to work and you can enjoy your afternoon off."

In the face of the prevailing good spirits, Thad could do nothing but go with the flow. Twyla had brought a boom box. Having been cautioned about Thad's dislike of country music, she'd also brought some truly awful rap tapes. Belva got tipsy on half a glass of champagne and started dancing, giving every male in the room a chance to be her partner—even a giggling Jeffrey.

It was when she had snagged Thad and was twirling him around the waiting area, that the room temperature seemed to drop about ten degrees. The music stopped abruptly and everyone froze, almost as if they were playing living statues. Thad, his back to the door, was the last to turn and see the newcomer who had so altered the mood.

Gilbert Foster, the Scanlon County Commissioner, stood just inside the door, looking scandalized from the roots of his sparse hair to the soles of his wingtips.

Six

Lindy resisted the urge to duck behind the soft drink fountain when she saw Thad enter the VFW hall that evening. He looked big and primal and all-male, but mostly he looked like a tightly corked bottle full of fury.

"Are you going to hand me that drink or dump it on the floor?" the woman standing in front of Lindy teased.

"Huh? Oh, sorry." Lindy relinquished her grip on the cola she'd been about to serve before Thad's entrance had distracted her.

"I don't blame you for staring," said Alice Quintana under her breath as her gaze followed Lindy's. Alice, a young phys-ed teacher at Winstonia's high school, was popular with the kids and one of their first choices as a chaperon for tonight's dance. "Mucho macho. You're one fortunate lady."

Lindy felt anything but fortunate as Alice wandered away with a parting wink. Even the realization that the whole county now considered Thad and her something of an item had little effect on her. She was too busy wondering how she would stand up in the face of his anger.

Though he stopped to speak to a few of the kids, he moved inexorably in her direction. He'd zeroed in on her location the moment he entered the hall, and he obviously didn't intend to let her escape.

She knew better than to smile when Thad approached. His eyes, normally as soft and smooth as melted chocolate, held a sharp, furious glint.

"I'd like a lemon-lime, please," he said, his voice tight.

So that's how it was going to be, Lindy thought as she filled a paper cup with ice. Civility edged with animosity.

She handed him the drink and launched her defense, feeble though it was. "Thad, what can I say? I'm sorry. How was I supposed to know the old fussbudget would show up for a surprise inspection?"

"You ran out on me," he said, leaving his drink untouched.

"Could we discuss this later?" she asked sensibly.

"When? When do we ever have any privacy?"

"Can we at least have one argument at a time?" she pleaded, praying no one else was eavesdropping.

As he stood staring at her, silently challenging her to give him a reason to lose his temper, Alice returned. She gave Lindy a questioning look. "Would you like me to take over here for a while?"

"Yes, thank you," Lindy replied, grateful to turn over the soft drink fountain. She wiped her sticky hands on a dish towel and grabbed her purse before joining Thad. "You want privacy? Follow me."

He did follow her, across the dance floor and out the door. It was a beautiful evening—warm, breezy, full of the overblown scents of a ripe summer. A perfect night for romance, she thought wryly. Unfortunately romance appeared to be the last thing on Thad's mind.

She led him all the way to the little park adjacent to the hall, far from prying eyes, and sat down at a picnic table. "Talk," she said. "Yell and scream if you want. Get it all off your chest."

He set his untouched drink on the picnic table and stared at her—hard. "You could have at least stuck around to face the consequences. But you're not very good at that, are you? You breeze through life leaving one disaster after another for someone else to clean up."

She counted to ten, then twenty. Thad wasn't the only one with a temper, and hers was being stretched to the breaking point. But a shouting match wouldn't accomplish anything except drive them further apart, and that wasn't what she wanted. With a jolt, she realized that she very much wanted to restore harmony between them. Thad had added a new dimension to her life. He'd become so essential, in fact, that she'd actually considered remaining in Corrigan awhile longer.

She had to admit that she cared for Thad—even if at the moment he was behaving like a horse's behind. That caring went beyond an initial fascination and an explosive physical attraction.

"Do you honestly think my continued presence would have helped matters?" she asked calmly. "Gilbert Foster despises me. Before he was county commissioner he was my high school principal, and we knocked heads every other week. I left you and Chet alone to deal with him because I thought it was the most sensible thing to do at the time."

But Thad obviously was not in the mood for sensible explanations. He'd worked up a good head of steam, and he was determined to vent it. "I could have lost my job," he said, pointing a finger in her face. "I'm sure you don't understand what that means, since you've never held a steady job in your life—" He stopped himself. Abruptly the fight went out of him. "I'm sorry, Lindy. That was uncalled for."

But the apology came too late. His assault on her character had hit its mark, causing a pain so sharp in her heart that she had to blink back tears. Tears! She hadn't cried real ones in years. "You're wrong, Thad," she said, her voice quavering. "I do understand what your job means to you. And you must know that I'd never purposely do anything to jeopardize it." She cleared her throat and managed to pull herself back together. "How much trouble are you in?"

He sighed, his storm of anger spent. "What would have normally been a thirty-minute, routine inspection became a four-hour ordeal. First it took an hour to explain what I was doing at the office dressed like a bum—" He stopped, and his face took on the most peculiar expression.

"What is it?" Lindy asked.

"I was just thinking of how it must have looked to Gilbert," he replied. "It must have been quite a shock to see the straitlaced sheriff wearing a silly hat and dancing with my dispatcher to that ridiculous music—" He stopped again, and then something happened that was nothing short of miraculous. Thad Halsey started laughing—not the small, controlled chuckles he normally indulged in, but an all-out belly laugh that almost shook the ground on which he stood.

Lindy started laughing, too, as relief washed over her. Perhaps he was actually going to forgive her.

"Did you see the look on his face?" Thad asked as he gasped for air between gales of laughter. "He turned so red, I thought his head was going to explode."

"He just stood there with his jaw hanging open, like he'd walked in on an orgy," Lindy said as tears streamed down her cheeks. Then she added, in a nasal, pompous voice, "'Just what in the Sam Hill is going on here?'" Her creditable imitation of the commissioner sent Thad into more guffaws.

As their laughter degenerated into sighs and occasional chuckles, Thad put his arms around Lindy and squeezed her tightly. "I'm sorry, Lindy. Nothing like this has ever happened to me before, and I just didn't know how to handle it. I had to blame someone, and you were the easiest target. But it wasn't your fault."

"It was my fault. I don't always think of the consequences when I do something impulsive. This won't hurt your record, will it?" she asked, suddenly serious.

"An official warning goes in my file," he answered, "because of the champagne. The warning will be removed if I keep my nose clean for six months."

"That shouldn't be a problem for you." She continued to hold him close, loving the feel of his hard chest pressed against her breasts, his smooth-shaven cheek against hers, his soft, thick hair beneath her fingertips. "And I'll stay out of the way. I won't come within a mile of the courthouse. Oh, Thad, you were right when you said I'd cause you nothing but trouble. I really am sorry."

"Shhh. That's enough. I'm the one who's sorry. I said some things I shouldn't have."

"Words in the heat of anger. All but forgotten." She tried for a smile and failed. All but forgotten, yes, but not quite. His accusations regarding her transient life-style had struck a raw nerve. She could still feel it throbbing, like a sore tooth, but she wanted to gently probe it later when she was alone.

He rubbed her back soothingly, and the mood between them changed subtly from friendly forgiveness to something much more potent—and dangerous.

She struggled to think of a ploy to lighten the mood, and succeeded. "Helluva birthday for you. I haven't even given you your present yet."

"A present?" He released her slowly, his hands lingering on her bare arms. "You didn't have to do that."

She reached inside her braided-rope purse and extracted a small box wrapped in white paper. "You might not like it," she warned him as she handed him the box.

Judging from the uncertainty and anticipation on his face, he wasn't accustomed to presents. Lindy wondered if anyone had bothered with birthdays when he was a child. She couldn't imagine what life would be like under those circumstances. Her mother had always indulged her every wish for her birthday.

Thad opened the box and stared for several uncomprehending seconds at the strip of red leather studded with rhinestones. Then he smiled. "For Freddy," he murmured.

"The tag has her name and your address and phone number, in case she ever gets lost," Lindy explained.

He arched one skeptical eyebrow. "If she got lost, do you actually think I'd want her back?"

"Of course you would. Admit it, Thad, you're crazy about that dog."

"I'm crazy for ever letting her through my front door. You were supposed to find a home for her," he reminded Lindy.

"I tried. Honestly, I did. I even put an ad in the paper. No one wants her."

Thad smiled and shook his head, laying the collar back in its box. "I took her to the vet yesterday for her shots. Dr. Wang said she thought Freddy was half rottweiler. Do you have any idea how big a rottweiler gets?"

Lindy shrugged. "Maybe the other half is Chihuahua," she reasoned. "C'mon, we better get back inside before the little monsters burn the hall down." She stood and threw the strap of her purse over her shoulder, but he prevented her from leaving with an insistent hand at her waist.

"Wait."

She paused, unable to guess what else was on his mind. But when she looked up into those clear, brown eyes, eyes that had the power to caress her almost as surely as his hands could, she knew.

"Have any plans after the dance?"

"I have to stay and clean up."

He sighed impatiently. "I should have guessed. Every time we're together, you somehow fix it so that we're either in a public place or surrounded by a crowd. How long are you going to avoid being alone with me?"

"And I thought I was being so clever," she murmured, evading his probing gaze.

"Why, Lindy? What are you afraid of?"

"You have to ask? I practically sizzle every time you touch me."

"I know." His voice was low, full of promise. "I can feel the heat, yours and mine. Between us I think we could generate enough power to light up the whole damn county. Don't you want to find out?"

She'd never heard a more sincere proposition. And she'd never felt such keen regret as she did at the prospect of turning it down. "I don't want to get involved with you on that level, Thad."

"Why not?"

Damn, but he asked difficult questions. "Because...I like you too much to let you get that tangled up with me."

"What the hell's that supposed to mean?" he asked with less than his usual patience.

"You said it yourself," she answered softly. "I breeze through life, causing one disaster after another for someone else to clean up. I'll move on, eventually, and I just don't want to leave your life in a shambles when I do. The less involved we get, the smaller the mess we'll create."

He nodded thoughtfully. "You're afraid you'll devastate me when you go?"

Well, he'd latched onto that concept pretty fast. She hadn't wanted to couch it in quite those words—they sounded so smug, so arrogant. But they were pretty near the truth, too, so she nodded in cautious agreement. "Love-'em-and-leave-'em Lindy. That was my nickname in high school. Unfortunately my capacity for constancy hasn't improved any. The few intimate relationships I've had have tended to explode in a distinctly messy way. I don't want to see that happen with us."

She'd just been as painfully honest as she knew how, and he had the bad grace to laugh. "Lindy, I appreciate the concern over breaking my heart, but I think it's misplaced. My track record in the romance department isn't any better than yours."

"Really?" Now, that surprised her.

"Really. Not that it's anything to brag about, but no woman has ever held my interest for longer than a few weeks. So if I were you, I'd stop worrying about *my* heart and look out for your own, instead."

He'd certainly put her in her place, she thought, scuffing her sandals in the red dirt. It had never occurred to her that Thad would tire of her before she could tire of him. It was a sobering thought. "Regardless of whose heart gets broken, it's still a mess—one I'd like to avoid."

Abruptly Thad looked as if he'd had enough discussion. Without warning he pulled Lindy into his arms and claimed her with a kiss that shoved aside all civility, all reason. His mouth was hard on hers, demanding, pleading.

There was no argument in the world that would be effective against his assault on her senses, and in that moment she didn't care. She opened her mouth and willingly accepted his insistent tongue. She breathed in his tantalizing male scent and felt she was inhaling his very essence. It fanned embers of longing deep inside her, embers that were never quite dead when he was around.

He wound his fingers through her thick curls, holding her a willing prisoner, though the passion alone would have kept her there, pressed against his hardness, wanting more, so much more. The intensity of her body's response to him was like nothing she'd ever experienced before, burning out of control, all the stronger for having been denied.

"Tell me you don't want me," he rasped against her hair.

"I can't. You know I can't."

"I want to make love to you. You have so much passion in you and I want it all. I want you lying beneath me. I want to look into your eyes while we're making love and see the fire, green fire...." He buried his face in her hair, unable to continue. He was babbling, but the force of his desire for this woman had unlocked something inside him, something so deep and primitive he hadn't even known it was there. What little control he'd maintained around her was fast disintegrating.

"When the dance is over..." she whispered.

That was all he needed to hear.

A door opened somewhere, allowing the blaring music from inside the hall to drift outside briefly. It was enough to remind Thad where they were. He loosened his grip on Lindy's body, kissed her lightly on the forehead and straightened her blouse as the unmistakable sound of approaching footsteps intruded.

"Sheriff?" The single word, spoken by Jimmy McGruder, dripped with apology.

Lindy turned her back on both men, her arms folded and head bent. Her slender shoulders trembled, and Thad could only assume that, since virtually nothing could embarrass her, she was fighting the same maelstrom of feelings and emotions that still had him reeling.

"What is it?" he barked at Jimmy.

"Sorry, Thad." The deputy's face was bright red. "I wouldn't have bothered you, but the Handy-Mart on Highway 10 was held up."

Thad cursed under his breath. "Lindy, I have to go."

She turned toward him and his heart lurched. Her face was filled with arrested passion. "I heard. Go. And be careful."

He hesitated one final second, wishing there was something he could say. But there wasn't, not now. He settled for touching her shoulder before he and Jimmy loped off.

He used the time in the patrol car to pull himself together, to banish images of Lindy from his mind so he could concentrate on his work. Though he'd dealt with violent crimes on a nightly basis when he'd worked in Dallas, armed robberies weren't a common occurrence in Scanlon County. This one, at least, wasn't as bad as it could have been. Though a good amount of cash had been stolen from the small convenience store, no one was hurt.

By the time he'd taken the investigation as far as he could that night, it was three o'clock in the morning. He briefly considered going to Lindy's, then ruled out the idea. When he made love to her the first time, it damn sure wasn't going to be when he was mentally and physically exhausted.

"Hell," he muttered as he pulled the pickup into his driveway. He hated to admit it, but it was probably a good thing his work had intruded. He'd never in his life pushed a reluctant woman into bed, and he didn't particularly want to start with Lindy. Whatever her reasons were, valid or no, she wasn't ready.

As late as it was, as tired as he was, he didn't go to bed. Instead, he walked down to the lake, with Freddy trailing after him, and stood on the dock staring out over the moonlit water. He wanted Lindy with a force that was like nothing he'd ever felt. But he wanted her without reservations. Whatever happened between them in the long run, he didn't want her to regret their physical love.

He'd have to wait, dammit. But for Lindy, he could.

Lindy straightened her apartment and put fresh, scented sheets on the bed when she got home from the dance, though she didn't really expect him to show up. Dealing with the convenience store holdup might occupy him well into the wee hours, and work would always come first for Thad.

By 2:00 a.m., she convinced herself that he definitely wasn't coming. She turned out the lights and climbed into her big, empty bed. But still she lay awake, listening for the sound of his truck, or his footfall on the creaky stairs. Her body, tense with unleashed desire, still ached for completion.

When she awoke the next morning her muscles were tight and sore from the tension. Her stomach sank as she rose from the bed and acknowledged that Thad hadn't even called. That put her in a surly mood. For someone who professed to want her body beyond all reason, he'd certainly been easily distracted.

With her eyes still heavy-lidded from lack of sleep, she peered into her empty refrigerator, then sighed in disgust. She didn't have anything remotely edible in the whole apartment. She'd have to mooch breakfast off her mother.

A few minutes later she was sitting alone at Marianne's kitchen table, munching on cereal and scanning the pages of a college course catalog that had arrived in yesterday's mail, addressed to Claire. Nothing piqued her interest quite like the prospect of a new and different subject to study. Meteorology? Astronomy? How about medieval poetry? It was an exercise in futility, she realized. She wouldn't be here long enough to complete any course.

Halloween. She'd be gone by Halloween.

"Oh, you're here," said Marianne as she entered the kitchen, her heels clicking on the tiled floor. She'd undoubtedly been up for hours doing something worthwhile. "I was getting ready to call you. Something just came for you."

"Something like what?"

"Something like flowers."

"Flowers!" Cold cereal quickly lost its appeal. Lindy jumped up from her chair, then forced herself to walk not run, to the table in the entry hall. There sat a small but exquisite arrangement of birds-of-paradise.

For a moment, she could only stare at it in unmitigated delight. Not daisies. Not roses or carnations. Birds-of-paradise.

"Aren't you going to open the card?" asked Marianne, who had followed expectantly on Lindy's heels.

Lindy had to squint to read the small writing that had been squeezed on to the tiny florist's card:

These flowers were picked when they were ready to bloom, and not a moment sooner. To cut them any earlier might have diminished their beauty.

The card wasn't signed.

For the second time in twenty-four hours, tears sprang into Lindy's eyes. The big, bad sheriff had the soul of a poet. He was telling her in his own way that he was willing to wait to make love, until she was emotionally ready and the time was perfect.

"What does it say?" Marianne demanded impatiently.

Lindy laughed, dashing her tears away with the back of her hand. "Only the most romantic thing anyone's ever said to me."

Marianne looked skeptical. "Thad? Romantic? Oh, no, Lindy, you've got that look in your eye. You've really fallen for him, haven't you? And, dear Lord, he's fallen for you. No man spends that kind of money on flowers unless he's smitten."

Instead of arguing the point, Lindy changed the subject. "Mother? I think I'd like to take a couple of courses at Stephen F. Austin this fall."

"What? Oh, that's a nice idea," Marianne agreed blandly. "Can you afford the tuition?"

Lindy grimaced. "I was hoping you might volunteer to further my education."

Marianne laughed humorlessly. "Lindy, dear, I've spent your college fund three times over on your education, and I have yet to see even the glimmer of hope for a degree. No, I'm afraid you'll have to handle your own tuition. And don't look at me like I'm an ogre. I'm letting you live in the garage apartment rent-free. What more do you want?''

"Paint," Lindy answered succinctly as she gathered up her flowers and the course catalog. Then she gave her mother a kiss on the cheek. "I think I'll fix up the apartment a bit.''

Marianne sighed. "I have a charge account at Builder's Corner. You can get the paint there.''

"Thanks." Lindy smiled serenely as she went back to her apartment. She was a little surprised that her mother had balked at paying the tuition. Short of an outright cash loan, Marianne seldom refused her daughter any request.

Still, Lindy wasn't discouraged. She'd just have to dip into her savings for the tuition money. Education was an investment, after all.

The charcoal was burning nicely, the chicken well-marinated. Thad was stocking his refrigerator with wine and soft drinks when he heard the unmistakable roar of Lindy's Cadillac in the driveway.

He was glad she was early, he thought as he closed the refrigerator door and went to greet her. He'd have her all to himself—at least until Kevin and Twyla arrived for their canasta game, which had preempted the usual all-male poker game this week. And because he hadn't seen Lindy since the dance almost a week ago, his hands itched to touch her.

She barreled through the front door carrying a large, foil-covered pan in front of her like a shield. "Hi." She deftly dodged his kiss, so that it landed in the air next to her cheek. "I'll just take dessert into the—''

He forcefully removed the pan from her grip and set it on the hall table, then grasped her shoulders and pulled her roughly against him.

Her mouth barely had time to register a surprised O before it met up with his, but her reaction changed quickly from shock to rampant enthusiasm. She smelled like chocolate and tasted sweet and warm, like summer itself. The familiar heat rose up in him like a hot August sunrise.

Her lilac silk blouse was slick under his hands. She was as lean as a healthy female could be, and yet she still managed to feel soft and womanly. He let one hand slide around to cup her breast as his mouth strayed along her jaw and down her neck, finally settling at the base of her throat.

"Thad?" Her voice was a sultry whisper. "Won't Kevin and Twyla be here soon?"

"Any minute," he answered against her neck. "That's why I didn't waste any time."

"But..."

Reluctantly he moved his hand from her breast and retreated from the assault on her neck, so he could see her face. He cupped her chin in one large hand. "I know I promised, in my own, oblique way, not to push you, Lindy. And I won't. But I didn't promise to keep my hands completely off you. This is not, and never will be, a platonic relationship. I just wanted to be sure you understood that."

He left her staring after him, weak-kneed and limp, as he carried the pan into the kitchen, whistling a phrase from some classical piece that she recognized but didn't know the name of. "What's in here, anyway?" he called over his shoulder.

The man would be the death of her! "It's something my mother made," she answered, pulling herself together as she followed him into the kitchen.

"Chocolate, right?"

"Among other things. How did you know?"

He gave her a mischievous smile as he peeled back the foil, revealing one disturbed corner of the whipped-cream-topped dessert. "Just as I thought. You sampled it on your way over."

He must have tasted the evidence, she realized, touching her lips.

"Want something to drink?" he asked, nodding toward the refrigerator. "There's cold root beer, and also a bottle of wine."

"I'll get it," she volunteered, anxious to occupy her hands. "How about something for you?"

"I'd like some wine, thanks," he said, moving toward the patio door. "I'd better go tend the fire."

Now that you've already built a fire in here, she added silently. She shook her head and quietly acknowledged that she was out of her mind to resist the man's sex appeal. He wouldn't push her. He was too honorable to do that. But he wasn't above seducing her in a thousand subtle little ways, until she fell to her knees begging him to make love to her.

The end result was inevitable, she thought as she poured chilled chablis into one of the stemmed glasses he'd left on the counter. Unless she broke things off here and now, she and Thad would end up in bed. Their relationship had to move forward or die, and she wasn't about to let it die. She was torturing herself and him for no good reason.

"Atta way to rationalize it, Lindy," she congratulated herself wryly as she popped the top on her soft drink can.

She was about to take the wine outside to him when the phone rang. Seeing that he was busy tending the charcoal, she picked it up herself. "Halsey residence," she said soberly, in case the call was official.

"Since when did Thad get an answering service?"

"Oh, Kevin, it's you. Hey, you're supposed to be on your way over. The coals are hot and the wine is cold. Get a move on!"

"Uh, that's what I'm calling about. We can't come."

"What?" she said, more sharply than she meant to.

"Jeffrey came down with poison ivy, head to toe. He's miserable, and Twyla doesn't want to leave him. Sorry, sis. I know it's the last minute...."

"It's way past the last minute!" she said indignantly.

"What are you complaining about? Put the leftover chicken in the fridge and finish off the wine. I'm sure, left to your own devices, you can think of something creative to do with your time."

"That's not funny, Kev." It was also all too accurate.

He laughed anyway. "Let me talk to Thad."

"No. You'll just make some lewd, embarrassing sugges-tion. I'll give him your sincere regrets." She started to hang up when she remembered Jeffrey. Her voice softened. "Hey, remember when you used to get poison ivy and I'd play checkers with you, hour after hour, to keep your mind off the itching?"

"Yeah, I remember," Kevin said. "That's a good idea. I'll try to find a checkerboard."

After they hung up, Lindy opened the patio door with her elbow, Thad's wine in one hand and her soft drink in the other. Freddy met her, jumping ecstatically.

"Down," Thad said sharply.

The pup immediately dropped to the deck, wagging her tail and looking expectantly at Thad for further directions. Thad looked smug.

"I'm impressed," Lindy said. "My, that's a handsome collar she's wearing. Good heavens, she's *huge.*"

"And not even three months old yet."

"Seems the two of you have come to an understanding." Lindy surveyed the unfenced backyard leading down to the lake. "Won't she run away?"

"Hah. I should be so lucky." But he smiled fondly at the mutt. His smiles came more easily now than they had a few weeks ago. Lindy wondered if he really was happier, or if he'd just learned to trust her enough to let her see him smile.

"Kevin just called," she said, handing him the wine. "It seems Jeffrey got into poison ivy and Twyla doesn't want to leave him with a sitter."

Thad raised one eyebrow. "They're not coming?"

She shook her head.

"And you're not running for the door?"

"Why should I?" she asked innocently, though her heart vibrated wildly. "I trust you, and myself. There's no reason we can't have a civilized dinner, just the two of us."

"I'm awfully glad to hear you say that." He touched her hair, then ran his index finger along her cheek before dropping his hand. "Otherwise, I'd have to eat almost four pounds of chicken by myself."

They did manage to put a serious dent in the tender charcoal-broiled chicken as they sat at the redwood picnic table, watching the sun set over Arrowrock Lake. Freddy lay at Thad's feet, accepting the occasional handout but otherwise not making a pest of herself. There was no escaping the Texas heat in August, but a breeze off the lake made it feel quite comfortable.

"I can see why you like it here so much," Lindy said as she watched a pair of ducks glide into the protected cove. "I've always liked the lake for boating and water skiing and keg parties on the beach, but I usually don't appreciate how peaceful it is."

"I suspect you don't stand still long enough to appreciate peaceful things very often. Now, I meant that as a compliment," he added quickly when she looked like she might take umbrage. "Really. You're the most...*alive* person I've ever met."

She could feel heat rising in her face. He'd taken a simple statement and made it sound like a verbal caress.

Thad ran his thumb lightly up and down her forearm. "So, would you like to go to a movie?"

The question surprised her. "I thought we were going to play cards," she said before she realized he'd been trying to give her a graceful escape.

He shrugged. "Fine by me. I don't much care for two-handed canasta, though. What else can you play?"

They stood and began cleaning up the leftovers.

"Spades?" she suggested. "Hearts?"

"We need more than two people," Thad argued.

"Casino? Spoons? Double solitaire?" But none of those elicited any enthusiasm.

"You play poker?" he asked as he opened the patio door for her.

She brightened. "Sure. My dad taught me when I was five."

"You must be pretty good, then."

"Fair," she admitted cagily. "You?"

"I do all right." But he had a wicked gleam in his eye.

After the leftovers were put away, Thad went to get the cards and the poker chips while Lindy served up two huge globs of the decadent dessert she'd brought. She took the plates and forks to the exquisite teak and green-felt card table, set up in a corner of the large living room. Thad was already distributing equal portions of beautifully carved wooden poker chips.

"Why do I get the feeling I've been hustled?" she said, eyeing the two brand-new decks of cards. "You're no amateur."

"We could go back to canasta," he suggested.

"No way. I'm still gonna wipe up the table with you."

"You sound pretty sure about that. Care to make the game a little more interesting?"

"I don't play for money," she said cautiously. "For one thing, I don't have any."

"I wasn't talking about money." He leaned over the table until he was nose to nose with her. "Why don't we play strip poker?"

Seven

At first she laughed. "Thad!" But when he continued to stare at her, unsmiling, she had to believe he was serious. So he knew something about having fun and taking risks, after all. Where was her serious, stodgy, *safe* sheriff?

"So, I shocked *you* for a change," he said when she made no further reply. "Come on, what are you worried about? If you're such a good poker player, I'll be sitting here buck naked and you'll still be fully clothed."

The image he painted wasn't without some appeal. And the challenge he issued couldn't be ignored. "That's right," she said with a confident smile. "I wasn't the champion poker player in my dorm without good reason."

"Ha! Which college?"

"All of them. Where did you come by your expertise, pray tell?" she asked as they settled into chairs on opposite sides of the table.

"In a pool hall. I was seven years old. By the time I was sixteen I could earn more at cards than I could frying hamburgers. Poker winnings financed my way through the police academy.''

Her smile deserted her. She was sunk. She knew it, but that didn't concern her as much as the brief reminder of how harsh his childhood must have been. She was saddened by the thought of an unkempt little boy hanging out at pool halls because no one cared enough to forbid him to do it. She was also warmed by the fact that he finally trusted her enough to share with her a tiny part of the past, which he kept so carefully locked away.

He shuffled the cards, then shoved the deck toward her so she could cut them. "Five card draw. Nothing wild."

Lindy squelched her softer side and applied herself to cutthroat poker. Soon, however, it became obvious that luck was on Thad's side. After several minutes of intense play he still wore far too many clothes for her taste. In fact, all he'd taken off was his watch and one boot. She, on the other hand, had removed earrings—one at a time—necklace, watch, both sandals and her belt.

If she lost one more hand, she'd have to remove something significant. Judging from Thad's warming gaze, he was anticipating that very moment. Her nipples tightened beneath her silk blouse.

She slowly fanned the cards she'd been dealt, and exhaled as she did. Three queens. This hand was almost in the bag. Her mind was already skipping ahead to what article of clothing Thad might be induced to remove.

Holding on to the queens, she placed her rejected cards facedown on the table. "Two."

Thad fulfilled her request, studied his own hand, then dealt himself three new cards. "Okay, lady, let's see whatcha got." They'd long since done away with the formalities of betting chips. The final outcome of each hand was much more interesting.

"Read 'em and weep," she said, laying out her queens.

A dangerous smile spread slowly across his face as he placed his cards on the table with a flourish. "Full house beats three-of-a-kind."

Lindy stared at the cards for at least ten seconds before reacting. "You have the most incredible luck of anyone I've ever played with. No matter how good my hand is, yours is always better."

"You're procrastinating," he said casually. Only the tiny muscle twitching in his jaw gave any indication of his true interest in the proceedings.

She scooted her chair back and stood up. If she was going to perform a striptease, she damn sure wasn't going to do it sitting down. She reached for the top button of her blouse and flipped it open, staring defiantly at him.

She'd never stood before a man and taken off her clothes with the lights on. She found the prospect incredibly arousing. Or maybe it was simply the thought of undressing for Thad Halsey that ignited her desire. Moistening her dry lips with the tip of her tongue, she reached for the second button.

"Wait."

Her hand froze.

Thad folded his arms on the table and laid his head in them. "I can't believe I'm saying this, but you don't need to go through with it."

She should have been relieved he was letting her off the hook. Instead, she felt a crushing disappointment. "I don't welsh on my bets," she said indignantly. She flicked open the second button, then the third. She pulled the lilac blouse's hem free of her purple cotton shorts, and the last button gave way.

She stood very still and waited. If he changed his mind—if he turned her away—she wouldn't know how to handle it. She wanted Thad to make love to her, more than she'd ever wanted anything.

Thad raised his head just enough that he could peek up at her over his forearms. The open blouse revealed a tantalizing glimpse of golden skin. His stomach muscles tightened as he visualized his hands slipping inside the blouse, pushing the pale silk off her shoulders and down her slender arms.

Her actions mirrored his fantasy. Slowly she parted the front of the shirt and let it slide to the floor, revealing a tormenting bit of white lace that barely whispered across her dark pink nipples.

He'd never intended for things to go this far. He had no idea whether she was issuing an invitation or merely too proud and stubborn to back down.

"Your deal," he said, sitting up and forcing his gaze to her expressive green eyes. He found them as exciting as any other part of her, however, so he looked over her shoulder and focused on a lamp, one he didn't particularly like.

"How about we try a new game?" she responded, her words a tremulous whisper.

That left no doubt as to her intent. He'd been prepared to wait much longer for this moment, and her unexpected invitation sent a bolt of desire charging through his body. Suddenly the card table separating them seemed as long and wide as a football field. Before Thad could decide whether to go under, over, or around it to get to her, she was standing by his chair.

"There's something I've been dying to know," she said as he stared up at her, momentarily torn between an all-consuming desire to possess her and a paralyzing fear that he'd do or say something wrong and shatter this fantasy come to life.

"What's that?" He allowed himself to touch her, laying one hand flat against her midriff. To simply feel her breathing was incredibly stimulating.

"Are you tan *all over?*"

"Are you?" he countered as he reached behind her with both hands and unclasped her bra. She wasn't. As he freed her of the delicate undergarment, he revealed a thin strip of ivory skin across her breasts, where the sun hadn't touched her.

Her breasts were perfect, small but firm and high, with nipples the color of tight pink rose buds. His inhibitions pushed rudely aside, he reached up and brushed his thumb over one of the taut peaks. Encouraged by her slight intake of breath, he turned in his chair until she was standing between his thighs, then drew the hard bud into his mouth.

She tasted as sweet as she smelled. As he licked and nibbled, she began to knead his shoulders with surprisingly strong hands. Her breathing became more pronounced. He could actually feel her heartbeat fluttering erratically against his mouth.

When she let out a little whimper, he slowed his efforts for fear she would come apart before they'd even gotten started. "Easy, darlin'," he murmured, coaxing her into his lap. "We have all night."

Her breath came in quiet, quick gasps as she leaned her head against his neck. "I can't believe what you do to me," she whispered.

"The feeling's mutual," Thad murmured in agreement. As many times as he'd fantasized about it, nothing had prepared him for the pure, white-hot excitement gripping his body.

Without warning he stood and scooped her into his arms. The bedroom was too damn far. After a split second's deliberation, he carried her to the sofa and layed her gently onto the nubby white cushions. Finding his clothes too confining to abide another moment, he kicked off his one remaining boot, peeled off his shirt, stepped out of his crisp jeans. All the while he undressed, his eyes never left Lindy's face.

This far from the lamp, he could still make out her blatantly aroused expression. Her clear green gaze followed each movement of his hands, and was now focused quite unselfconsciously on his blue silk boxer shorts.

"You're full of surprises tonight, aren't you, Sheriff?" she asked, sitting up to lightly touch the fabric. Every nerve in his body pulsed as her hand came near his obvious arousal. "Silk. Silk underwear. That's incredibly sexy."

He wore silk for practicality, not to be sexy; there was no cooler fabric in the summer. But why should he point that out? "I'm glad you like them," he said honestly.

"I'd like them better if they were somewhere besides on you," she shot back with a mischievous smile.

"Happy to oblige." He looked her straight in the eye as he quickly dispensed with the boxers. Then he sat beside her and went to work on what remained of her clothing. But his hands shook so much that she had to take over. She unfastened her shorts and tugged them over her hips, revealing pristine white cotton.

"Not quite what I would have guessed, either," he said as he leaned down and planted a warm kiss on her abdomen.

But clearly she was no longer in the mood for banter. She sucked in a gulp of air and closed her eyes, then wilted back against the cushions. He leaned over her and lightly kissed the corner of her mouth as he tucked his fingers under the elastic around her hips and slid the cotton down her satiny legs.

The time for leisurely preliminaries was past. He kissed her in earnest. Her response, as always, was instantaneous and fiery, until trying to hold her was like holding a live flame in his arms. She made anxious little noises in the back of her throat as her kisses and caresses became bolder. Her passion at full-throttle had more horsepower than the V-8 under the hood of her infernal red Cadillac.

They found the couch too confining and rolled onto the carpet, where their volatile loveplay could have free rein.

Lindy was a wild creature, exciting him to a fever pitch then pulling back, murmuring sweet endearments into his ear one moment and thrillingly explicit words the next. Her hands urged and soothed, sometimes gentle as butterfly wings, sometimes unbelievably strong.

With no trace of shyness she stroked his shaft and just about sent him through the roof. "I can't wait any longer," she whispered urgently.

He groaned and then pulled her insistent hand away from him, where it could do no harm. "You're speeding again," he said with a low chuckle.

"So write me a ticket later." She was suddenly all arms and legs and sweet, hot desire, writhing beneath him as he kissed her mouth once again. "I want you *now*."

He was only too ready to meet her demand, but she was so agitated that he couldn't get her to lie still long enough for him to take the next logical step. She wasn't playing coy; she was operating on pure animal instinct. Finally he pinned her to the carpet with his body, held her arms above her head, and nudged her legs apart with his knee.

"Yes?" he rasped, poised to sheath himself in her, prolonging the exquisite anticipation for as long as possible.

"Yes!" she groaned with shocking need.

Instead of plunging into her as impulse dictated, he entered her slowly, letting her take him inch by inch and watching the play of expressions on her face.

"Yes, yes, yes, *please.*" She tugged at her bottom lip with her teeth and closed her eyes, her head lolling back and forth.

Her total lack of control was just about the most endearing thing he'd yet discovered about her. Never, ever, had he made love with a woman who could so abandon her inhibitions. She made him feel like the best lover she'd ever had, the best lover *any* woman had ever had, and he'd be damned if he'd disappoint her.

Once he was buried in her warmth, he could have let go at any time, he was that ready, but he held off. He closed his eyes for a moment, centered his concentration, and then began to move, very slowly.

She opened her eyes and treated him to the most beatific smile he'd ever seen as she wrapped her long legs around his thighs. He slipped one hand under her hips and pulled her against him, driving even more deeply into her.

"More, faster, oh *please* Thad, don't stop, don't stop—" Her eyes flew open and her mouth formed a surprised O. He could feel her slipping over the edge, tightening around him. Then she began to laugh, a high, sweet sound with the clarity of a bell. It was so beautiful that it gripped his heart, and then his stomach, and then he too let go, pouring himself inside her.

The moment of ecstasy seemed to last forever.

When next Thad was fully conscious of reality, he lay beside Lindy, holding her against him, and she was crying instead of laughing.

"Oh, God, Lindy, what's wrong?" he asked as fear gripped his belly. "Did I hurt you?"

"Nothing's wrong," she assured him, sniffling against his chest. "It was just so beautiful. Something came over me and I...I can't describe it."

Relief washed over him. "You don't have to describe it," he said, stroking her hair. He'd seen it in her face, felt it in his own heart. "Is it always like this for you?" he couldn't help asking. He didn't like thinking of her with other lovers, but he had to know if this was simply the way she made love, or if it was something they'd created together, something unique. Either way, no sex had ever been this good for him.

"I can guaran-damn-tee you, nothing's *ever* been like this," she said fiercely. "Do you think this was a one-time lucky deal, like a shooting star?"

He ran a hand down her side and over her smooth hip. "One way to find out."

She laughed and looked into his eyes, then reached up to smooth an unruly curl from his forehead. She'd actually been worried that his lovemaking might be as reserved as the rest of him. What a ridiculous notion. He was incredibly responsive, and instinctively knew exactly when to kiss her, where to touch her. He'd had her on the verge of climax from just kissing her breast.

"Will you spend the night with me?" he asked.

She nodded.

"Would you like to move to the bedroom?"

She shook her head. "It's not even ten o'clock yet."

"I wasn't suggesting we sleep. Ah, I know. How about if I draw you a nice warm bath?"

What a treasure, she thought delightedly. A man who knew how to love her and then pamper her. "Only if you join me. No, wait. I have a better idea. You have that big, beautiful lake right out your back door. Let's go swimming."

He smiled at that, then frowned. "Did you bring your suit?"

"Oh, Thad, puh-leeze. You are hopelessly provincial sometimes. Why do we need suits?"

"You mean skinny-dipping?" He laughed. "No way."

Lindy sat up, resisting his attempts to cuddle her. Now that she'd voiced the idea, she was committed to it. "Your neighbors on one side are out of town. You don't have neighbors on the other side. It's dark, we're in a secluded cove, so who could possibly see us?" She hopped up and pulled him with her, then scampered for the back door with Thad in hot pursuit.

"Let me at least turn out the floodlight," he called after her as she slipped out the door. The light went off, plunging the backyard into darkness.

Guided only by moonlight, she picked her way through the grass, dodging from tree to tree like a wood nymph. Freddy frolicked along with her, enjoying the chase. She could hear Thad's surefooted steps behind her, closing the distance between them, but she made it to the dock before he could catch her. She raced to the end of the planking, then threw up her hands and twirled around in sheer delight.

"Isn't this wonderful?" she declared.

Thad had stopped just short of colliding with her, then stared at her like she'd lost her mind.

"Get with the program!" she said. "Without clothes we're more in tune with nature. Feel the wind against your body, Thad? See the moonlight reflected on our skin?"

Without warning he picked her up. "Feel the water closing over your head, Lindy?" he said as he tossed her unceremoniously into the lake.

She came up sputtering to find him standing on the dock laughing. Freddy ran up and down the planks, barking at the commotion.

"What did you do that for?" Lindy asked.

"Because, you're too damn perky for your own good, and every once in a while you need to be taken down a peg." He softened the criticism with a smile. "Wait there, I'll be right back." He disappeared into the small boat house at the end of the dock, and emerged a moment later with an inflated raft. He sailed it into the water, then dived in after it.

He wasn't tan all over, Lindy noted. She'd been too agitated before to notice. She felt a certain sense of satisfaction at finally knowing the answer.

They shared the raft, leaning their elbows on it from opposite sides. Thad reached up, cupping her cheek in his hand, and kissed her—not with the passion of a few minutes ago, but with a tenderness that brought a tightness to her throat. "Just for the record," he said, "I did notice the moonlight on your skin."

They floated lazily in the water for more than an hour, talking in drowsy voices, touching often, taking time for slow, leisurely caresses, which they'd been in too much of a hurry before to enjoy.

At one point Lindy rested her chin on her forearms and looked up at Thad. "How long have we been going out?"

"Almost a month, I think."

"That's a long time. Are you getting tired of me yet?"

He snorted. "Not hardly. Why, are you bored?"

She shook her head and laughed. Beneath the raft, her feet found his. She curled her toes against his calf, enjoying the solid feel of him. "Do you think we could make love in the water?" she asked, trapping his legs between hers and pulling his lower body closer.

"We could always try," he said lazily, reaching down behind him with one hand to grab her ankle. "But I think we might drown unless we—" He cut himself off, looking suddenly alert. "What was that?"

"What?" She didn't hear anything except crickets.

"That."

She strained her ears, and finally discerned the faint sound that had caught his attention. A woman's voice carried over the water: "And if you'd have remembered to fill the tank like you were supposed to, we wouldn't be in this fix."

A small bass boat appeared around the bend and headed into the cove. The motor wasn't running. Instead, its two occupants were paddling fiercely.

Lindy looked over at Thad. His face was frozen in an expression of horror. "Oh, *no.* "

"That's the Baumgartners, isn't it?"

"Shh! Yes. They live at the other end of Star Harbor, and they like to fish in my cove."

"So? What's wrong with that?"

"Nothing, except that Charles is a minister, Hilda is a Girl Scout leader, and we're not wearing any *clothes,*" Thad hissed.

"Oh." Lindy sank deeper into the water so that at least she was decently covered.

"They haven't seen us yet," he whispered. "Maybe they'll float on by."

"Look," said Hilda Baumgartner. "Thad Halsey's lights are on. I'm sure he wouldn't mind lending us some gas."

"He is the sheriff, after all," her husband agreed. "He's supposed to help folks in trouble."

Thad and Lindy allowed themselves to drift until they were almost under the dock.

"I sure hope he has some extra gas," Hilda said as the older couple rowed the boat ever closer, both of them breathing heavily.

"I don't think I can paddle all the way home."

When they reached the dock, Charles stood up and secured the boat with a rope, preparing to disembark.

Thad put his arm around Lindy's shoulders. "I have to say something," he whispered. "Otherwise they'll go right up to the back door, look inside, and see our clothes all over the living room."

Lindy snickered, earning herself a pinch on her bare behind. "Ouch! Cut that out."

"What was that?" Charles asked, cocking his hand to one ear. Freddy barked playfully as she peeked over the edge of the dock, giving away their hiding place.

Thad waded out into the open. "Down here," he said, sounding resigned.

Startled at first, Charles looked down into the water, then grinned broadly. "Well, howdy, Sheriff! Nice night for swimmin', sure enough."

Lindy could have continued to cower under the dock. She probably would have escaped the Baumgartners' notice. But she couldn't let Thad take the fall by himself this time. She

swam out into the open. "Hi, Reverend. Lindy Shapiro, remember me?"

"Why, sure! Just talked to your ma last week."

Thad shot her a murderous look.

Charles removed his fishing cap and scratched his bald-
ing head. "We're glad you're home, Sheriff, 'cause we need
to borrow some go-juice for the boat." He laughed self-
consciously. "Seems I forgot to fill the tank, and since it was
dark I didn't notice—"

"There's an extra five-gallon can in the boathouse,"
Thad said quickly. "Help yourself. Key's on the ledge over
the door."

"Don't mind if I do," Charles said with a grateful smile.
But when he turned and stretched his arm up toward the
ledge, he couldn't quite reach it. "Uh-oh, seems you're a
mite taller than me, Sheriff. Looks like I'll need some help."

There was a long, long moment of silence. "I'm afraid
that's not possible," Thad finally said. Even in the moonlight, Lindy could see that a blush darkened his tanned face.
"I'm not, um, wearing any clothes."

Lindy dropped her chin and bit down on her lip, trying
hard not to laugh.

"What'd he say?" asked Hilda.

"Said he's not wearing any—" Charles halted self-
consciously. "Uh, never mind, dear. Maybe I can reach the
key, after all."

After several heroic leaps into the air, the minister managed to flip the key out of its hiding place. He retrieved it
from the ground, opened the boathouse, found the can of
gas and refilled his empty tank in record time.

"I'll just leave the can here on the dock," he said, his
words tumbling over one another. "Hilda, see if you can get
the motor started. Much obliged, Sheriff, and nice to see
you, Lindy." The motor roared to life as Charles cast off.
Without a backward glance, he pushed forward on the
throttle, spun into a U-turn and sped out of the cove.

Lindy, unable to contain herself a moment longer, dissolved into near-hysterical laughter. Judging from the way Thad's nostrils flared, he did not share her amusement, but she couldn't control herself.

"Will you stop laughing?" he demanded. "This is not at all funny."

"Come on, lighten up," she scolded, reaching out to touch his face. But he ducked away from her hand and turned his back on her. "Thad..."

He obviously was not going to shake this off. He hoisted himself onto the dock and walked toward the house, unmindful of the water dripping off his magnificently sculpted body. Lindy, her elbows resting on the planks, watched him leave her with a shiver of apprehension. She didn't feel much like laughing now.

After a few more seconds she climbed out of the water herself and ran for the house. The night air felt cool against her skin: when she opened the sliding glass door, the blast of air conditioning made her shiver and brought goose bumps to every inch of her skin.

Thad met her in the living room with a towel, then headed back out to the deck where it was warm. She followed him, but decided she would have been better off enduring the air conditioning than the frosty waves emanating from Thad as he dried himself. Somehow, she got the feeling that he wasn't going to laugh about this incident any time soon.

She blotted the remaining water from her body, then wrapped her towel around herself and sank into a deck chair. "It's not the end of the world, Thad," she said quietly.

"That's easy for you to say," he retorted as he wrapped the towel loosely around his hips. "Your reputation isn't at stake."

"Excuse me?" She jumped out of the chair and moved to face him. Freddy sat and watched them, her gaze moving anxiously from one to the other. "You weren't out there alone," Lindy continued.

"At least the Baumgartners would have *thought* I was alone if you hadn't introduced yourself. You picked a helluva time to display your impeccable manners."

"I figured it wasn't fair for you to shoulder all the embarrassment. The swim was my idea, after all. Anyway, the point is, your reputation isn't the only one at stake."

"I don't know why you're concerned about your reputation. There's not a whole lot to protect, is there?"

She slapped him.

Before he could do anything but stare at her in surprise, gingerly touching his reddening cheek, she turned and ran inside, sliding the glass door closed so forcefully she was surprised it didn't shatter.

It immediately opened again. "Lindy, wait a minute—"

"Just don't even bother," she said as she moved around the room, picking up her clothes. "If that's all the respect you have for me then you can damn sure get along without me." She whisked past him and fled to the bathroom.

She never should have made love with him, she thought as she pulled on her clothes. Something went haywire inside a man's head after he'd been with a woman. Suddenly he thought he could say anything and she'd forgive him. Well, not this woman.

So she was a bit impulsive and flighty. That did not give Thad Halsey a license to annihilate her character.

"Lindy, I'm sorry." His muffled voice carried through the bathroom door. "You know I didn't mean it."

"I know nothing of the sort," she returned as she opened the door. "Look, Thad, maybe you just aren't cut out to be the fun-loving type. When you take risks, every once in a while you get caught with your pants down—figuratively speaking most of the time. If you can't handle the occasional unpleasant consequences with a sense of humor, then it's time you went back to your nice, safe, content life. Find

yourself a placid little farmer's daughter and marry her."
She had to force the last sentence out around the lump in her
throat. As she whisked past him again, intent on finding her
purse and escaping, her eyes filled with tears.

"Lindy, please," Thad pleaded as he followed her into the
living room. "I have a very hot temper. Usually I manage to
keep a lid on it, but tonight I didn't. I didn't mean to say
what I did—"

"You didn't mean to say it *aloud*," she corrected him as
she dug through her purse for her car keys. "Good night,
Thad, and goodbye."

Thad watched her go, feeling more helpless than he ever
had in his life. Freddy looked up at him anxiously, as if she
expected him to *do* something, but he knew it was no use
going after Lindy. In her present mood she wasn't likely to
soften toward him.

He walked dejectedly to the sofa and sank into it, calling
to Freddy as he did. But the dog seemed no more forgiving
than Lindy. She lay down on the carpet and stared at him
with big, accusing eyes.

Lindy had been trouble from the word go; she was also
the best thing that had ever happened to him.

He leaned back and stared up at the ceiling. "What the
hell have I done?"

Lindy made it almost all the way to the highway before
she had to pull over and give vent to her tears. A cold band
of pain wrapped itself around her heart, pulling tighter and
tighter, squeezing the life out of her. Nothing had ever hurt
like this. Not even when her father had died had she felt this
desolate, this completely alone.

She had no one to blame but herself. Thad couldn't help
being the person he was, any more than she could help who
she was. She had to give him credit for trying to do things
her way, but it just hadn't worked.

After a few minutes she calmed down enough that she
could drive. The wind dried her hair and her tears, but she

was still sobbing by the time she pulled into the driveway. She started up the garage apartment stairs, intending to throw herself on the bed and cry herself to sleep, but then she saw Marianne's bedroom light on.

She turned and walked toward the back door of the main house. She needed to talk to her mother.

"What on earth is wrong?" Marianne asked when she looked up from reading in bed to see Lindy hesitating in the open doorway.

"Just everything."

Marianne pushed aside her legal journal and scooted over, then patted the edge of the bed. "Come tell Mother all about it."

More than anything, Lindy wanted to fall into her mother's arms, the solace of her youth. Maternal warmth, unquestioning love and comfort, had never sounded more inviting. But for once Lindy needed more than mere comfort. Instead of sitting beside Marianne on the bed, she pulled up a chair.

"It's Thad, isn't it?" Marianne asked.

Lindy nodded as she sank into her seat. "I found out tonight that he has absolutely no respect for me. He thinks I'm a flake, an irresponsible flake with a reputation that's already so bad it can't be damaged any further."

Marianne's spine stiffened in outrage. "Did he say that?"

"In just about those words," Lindy said with a nod. Then she sighed. "Mother, you have to tell me the truth. Does everyone think I'm a flake?"

"Lindy, of course not! Dear heavens, child, you're special. Everyone who knows you, everyone who even *meets* you, can see that. From the time you were born people were enthralled with you. You were such a beautiful, loving child. You've never had to—" Marianne cut herself off.

"I've never had to do anything," Lindy finished for her. "I've always gotten by on looks and charm. But no one respects me. That's true, isn't it?"

"Lindy, honey, everyone *loves* you...."

Lindy stood and walked over to her mother's dresser, idly touching a Venetian glass dish. "Thanks for not lying. I needed to hear that." She turned toward the door, but her mother's voice stopped her.

"Will you at least stay until your birthday? I've already invited people to the barbecue."

"What makes you think I'm leaving?" Lindy returned before walking out the door.

Eight

"Mother really kicked out the stops," Kevin said to Lindy as he surveyed the sea of guests in the backyard. Lindy nodded numbly in agreement. Because this was the first birthday party Marianne had thrown for Lindy in years, everyone even remotely known to the Shapiros had been invited, along with their extended families.

The patio was festooned with paper lanterns, and the swimming pool glowed with floating candles. Lindy's sister Claire and her husband, Bobby, presided over the barbecue pit and a pile of shortribs. Kevin had even brought over one of his gentler horses and was giving rides to the kids.

Normally Lindy loved nothing better than a good old-fashioned birthday blowout. But on this particular evening, the party's festive atmosphere only served as an uncomfortable contrast to her dismal mood. Nothing during the last two weeks had kept her from brooding about Thad—not throwing herself into work at the nature center, nor planning the final two summer youth programs.

In the past, whenever a relationship had hit the skids, she usually moped around for a couple of days, feeling guilty because she wasn't more upset, and then she moved on.

This situation was entirely different—disturbingly so.

When she sat down at the picnic table with a paper plate piled with ribs, coleslaw, beans and potato salad, she looked at the food and felt queasy. Her appetite was nonexistent.

A shadow fell on her plate. She looked up to see Twyla sitting across from her, her large, dark eyes full of mischief.

"Hey, Lindy," she said, flipping her long hair over one shoulder. "So you and Thad are really history?"

"Uh-huh." *Not now, Twyla,* she wanted to say. Her friend had all the subtlety of a vulture, eager for a gory tidbit.

"I heard that your mom invited him to the party."

Lindy toyed with her potato salad, unable to muster any enthusiasm for it. "She sent out the invitations right before Thad and I went our separate ways," she admitted. "But I'm not worried. He wouldn't dare show up."

"I wouldn't be so sure of that. There are a lot of good-looking women here who wouldn't mind consoling him."

"You, for instance?" Lindy asked, just daring Twyla to give her an excuse to bare her claws.

Twyla assumed an innocent expression. "You don't mind, do you? After all, you just said—"

"Now you listen to me, Twyla Jessup," Lindy hissed, suddenly furious. "You keep your mitts off Thad Halsey. You know, I actually thought you'd changed since high school. And what about Kevin, anyway? I thought you two were thicker than—" She cut herself off, feeling like a complete fool when Twyla started laughing. "I've been had, haven't I?"

Twyla came around the table and gave Lindy a hug. "Just testing the waters. I was pretty sure you were still hung up on him. By the way, he *is* here, but I'll leave the consoling in your capable hands.''

"He's *here?*'' Lindy said, but Twyla just wandered off as if she hadn't heard.

Someone sat down next to her. She heard the bench squeak, felt the warmth of a large male body. Slowly she turned her head, steeling herself for the encounter, but even then the initial sight of him took her breath away. Khaki slacks emphasized the lean lines of his thighs, and the lantern light picked out gold flecks in his brown eyes.

"Nice shirt,'' she said, letting her gaze drift over the gold-and-brown cotton. "Pretty wild print, though.''

"Oh, you know us fun-loving, risk-taking guys. We'll wear anything.''

"Why'd you come?''

He laughed uneasily. "Because I couldn't stay away from you any longer.''

"So you're physically attracted to me,'' she snapped. "Control it.''

"There's more to it than that, and you know it.'' He paused, obviously struggling to tamp down the flash of anger she'd provoked in him. When he spoke again his words were calm, deliberate. "Look, Lindy, if I thought apologizing would do any good, I'd do it. I'd do it standing on my head. I'd make a public announcement of it. I'd—''

"That's not necessary,'' she cut in. "I know you're sorry. I know you didn't hurt me intentionally. You were angry and you struck blindly, just like I did when I hit you.'' Filled with shame at the memory of the slap, she reached up to touch his face. The moment she realized what she was doing, she jerked her hand back, but not before she witnessed the longing she'd unwittingly stirred up in him.

She turned her gaze away, but some of her stubborn resistance was already crumbling away, like a fragile sea wall in the face of a gale. Why did he have to be so damn sincere? "Do you want to take a walk?'' she asked tentatively.

"Yeah, let's do that." Thad allowed hope to well up inside him as he swung his legs over the bench and stood, taking Lindy's hand. She resisted his touch at first, then relented with a sigh. He noticed Marianne Shapiro watching with undisguised interest as he and Lindy left the backyard and headed down the driveway toward the quiet, tree-lined street.

They walked without talking for a few minutes, letting the evening stillness settle around them. Finally Thad stopped and leaned against a parked car. He tried to put his arm around Lindy's waist and draw her close, but she didn't allow it.

"We both said some very harsh things," he said. "Can't we put them behind us? We have too much going for us to just dash it away."

She shook her head. "I can't pretend it never happened—no, wait," she said when he started to argue. "Remember the Fourth of July?"

He nodded hesitantly.

"I said some stupid, careless things that night, but they made you take a hard look at your life. Even though I was angry, and I was flinging out words without much thought, you saw some grain of truth in what I said. Remember?"

He nodded again, uncomfortable with the direction of her logic.

"Well, the same thing happened that night at your house. It was like a punch between the eyes. Suddenly I saw me the way you see me—irresponsible, irreverent, undisciplined—"

"Lindy, that's not how I see you!" Thad objected.

"On some level it is," she insisted. "Look at you, Thad. You started with nothing, you decided what you wanted and you went after it. You *became* someone. How could you possibly respect me when I started with every advantage and have done absolutely nothing with my life?"

"There is nothing wrong with your life," Thad said quietly. "And I do respect you—your compassion, your enthusiasm, your...your utter fearlessness. Maybe you're not perfect, but Lord knows I'm not, either. I have no room to criticize."

In the face of what Thad thought was an extremely persuasive argument, Lindy remained staunchly silent.

"Just tell me what you want," he finally said, frustrated almost beyond reason. "What can I do to convince you to give us another chance?"

She smiled up at him wistfully. "You've done more than enough. You've made an honest attempt to change some things in your life. Now it's time for me to make a change."

She's leaving, he thought, fighting a tightness in the back of his throat. "Dammit, you can't—" He clamped his mouth shut. He'd promised himself he would not lose his temper with her—ever. Not ever again. After taking a deep breath he made another attempt. "Lindy, I don't want you to go. Won't you think about it?"

She looked up at him again, more sharply this time. "What makes you think I'm leaving?" But her surge of belligerence was brief. "Don't you believe I'm capable of making a change that doesn't involve moving to another state?"

Thad wilted in relief against the parked car. She wasn't leaving, at least not yet. He pulled her against him; surprisingly, she didn't resist. "Don't scare me like that. I'm not near ready to let you go. And I'm sure you can make any kind of change you put your mind to, although personally I'll take you just the way you are."

He touched one finger to her chin and turned her face toward his. Then his mouth found hers as he sought an understanding that words couldn't seem to reach. And as they leaned against the dusty car and kissed in the darkness he thought he found it. The hope inside of him blossomed, filling his every fiber, and for the first time he fully acknowledged the powerful feelings he harbored for this woman—this very special woman who could anger him so thoroughly one minute, and the next, stir his soul with the most tender, gentle emotions.

He hesitated to put a name to those feelings. All he knew for sure was that they were there, and they weren't going away any time soon. Was there any chance he could convince Lindy to stay with him for as long as the feelings did?

She broke the kiss and took a deep breath, then leaned her head on his shoulder. "Sheriff, you don't give up easy, do you?"

"Nope. You can send me packing, but I'll be back." He paused, waiting for a reaction to that, but she remained silent. "Well? Are you going to?"

"Send you packing?" She gave a long, elaborate sigh, and then laughed. "No, I suppose not. I don't have that kind of willpower."

He released the breath he'd been holding, suddenly acutely aware of her warm body pressed against him. He wondered exactly how close she would allow him to get. He couldn't expect to just pick up where they left off, he supposed. It was more important than ever for Lindy to understand that he wanted much more than her body, fascinating though that was.

Even now, just holding her in a light embrace, his blood thrummed through his veins, whispering need to every cell. But he had to curb his tendency to push. As volatile as they both were right now, with their feelings so close to the surface, one unfortunate word or gesture and their fragile reconciliation might turn to so much dust.

"Maybe we should go back to the party," he suggested halfheartedly. "You are the guest of honor, after all, and I think we've invited enough speculation for one evening."

"You really hate that, don't you?" she asked as she reluctantly pulled away from him.

"Being the object of gossip? Yeah, I suppose I do."

"If you plan to hang around me, you'd better get used to it. I seem to garner more than my fair share...or maybe exactly my fair share," she amended. "I do sorta bring it on myself."

He stopped short of agreeing with her, reminding himself that Lindy wouldn't be Lindy if she weren't so cheeky.

She had been far too evasive lately, Thad decided suddenly one Wednesday evening as he was vacuuming out the inside of his truck. He'd seen Lindy only three times in as many weeks. Maybe he ought to push a little, he decided as he set the vacuum cleaner inside the garage. Her remaining time in Corrigan was slipping by at an alarming speed. It was already mid-September.

While the temperature still soared into the nineties during the day, the evening breeze bore a definite hint of autumn. As he barreled down the highway toward Corrigan, the smell of the wind made him think of what the future weeks and months would bring—falling leaves, warm cider, crackling fires in the hearth. He wanted to share all of those things with Lindy—if she'd ever take two minutes out of her busy schedule to see him.

He could understand her caution. He was being pretty cautious himself. But some other force was at work here. Something was distracting Lindy, making her busier than she ought to be. If he didn't know better, he'd think it was another man. But he did know better—didn't he? She wouldn't do that to him. Still, he was determined to find out what occupied so much of her time and attention.

"What are you doing here?" Lindy asked a bit ungraciously when Thad showed up at her door without warning. She softened the biting question with an uneasy smile. "I'm a mess."

"You're the best-looking mess I've ever seen," he said, giving her an appreciative once-over. If anything, her faded cutoff jeans, snug, paint-spattered T-shirt and tousled gold curls made her look soft and touchable.

"I guess since you're here, you'd like to come inside," she said, though she still stood blocking the doorway, her teeth worrying her lower lip.

"That's the general idea. Unless I'm...interrupting something?"

"Not exactly. Come on in." She sighed and stepped out of the way so he could enter the apartment. "Want something to drink?"

"Please. Water would be fine," he answered distractedly, surprised by the apartment's interior. As she disappeared into the kitchen to get his drink, he took a quick inventory. The walls had been painted a delicate eggshell. The windows sported new, pale peach curtains and valences. The mismatched furnishings now wore slipcovers in jaunty peach and cream stripes.

Then he noticed the books and papers strewn across the sofa and on the floor. He took a step closer and examined the open textbook. Calculus?

"Well, now you know my little secret."

He looked up to find her hesitating in the kitchen doorway. "Calculus?" he asked aloud.

"And statistics. And chemistry. Are you shocked?" She came toward him, holding out the glass of water.

"Relieved." He took the glass and drew a long sip. "I thought—never mind what I thought. It was too stupid. I'm just glad you have a legitimate reason for avoiding me. Why those particular classes?" he couldn't help asking.

She shrugged, and her eyes wouldn't meet his. "I don't know. Why do I do anything? I like school, I guess. Maybe that's why I never graduated. If I got a degree, I wouldn't have a reason to keep taking classes."

He didn't believe her. There was definitely a method to her madness, one she didn't want to reveal. He was fairly certain it had something to do with the comments she'd made the night of her party, when she'd talked about making changes.

Definitely encouraging. This was the first time Lindy had given him the slightest indication that she was capable of setting a long-term goal and then actually following through. Even the summer youth programs, which she'd so brilliantly initiated, she'd eventually turned over to Alice Quintana. If she completed this semester at school, perhaps she would convince herself to set other, more significant, more *ultimate* goals; maybe one of those goals would include him.

Suddenly uncomfortable with what he'd just admitted to himself, he gulped down the rest of his water and handed the glass back to Lindy. "You look busy. I'll leave you to your work."

He turned to go, but she stopped him with a tentative hand on his arm. "Why don't you stay for a little while?" she asked. "We really haven't seen much of each other lately."

"You have other priorities. Really, I don't want to interfere with your studying."

"I just have a few calc problems left to work, and then I'm done for the night," she said. "Honestly I could use a diversion."

His eyebrows shot up. "A diversion?" he said with mock outrage. "You wound me."

She looked immediately contrite over her choice of words. "I didn't mean—"

He cut off her apology with a swift, hard kiss. "I know. I'll stay for a while. Have you had dinner?"

She shook her head.

"Why don't I throw something together while you finish up your homework."

"You'll find some cold cuts in the fridge," she said with a grateful smile. "You can fix us a couple of sandwiches while I do these last three problems. It shouldn't take me too long."

When he came out of the kitchen a few minutes later balancing two thick ham-and-cheese sandwiches and two glasses of milk, he found Lindy sprawled on the couch on her stomach, chewing energetically on the end of her pencil as she punched numbers into a small calculator. A pair of tortoise-shell reading glasses were perched on the end of her nose.

"You can turn on the TV if you want," she said when he set the plates on the coffee table. "It won't bother me at all."

He could have made a snide comment about her study habits—hadn't she ever heard of good posture, bright light and no distractions? But he decided not to break her concentration. The sooner she got done with her homework, the sooner they could progress to... other things.

Instead of television, he selected a news magazine from her coffee table. Sitting at the end of the couch with Lindy's feet resting in his lap, he leafed through the magazine and munched on his sandwich. All the while he was conscious of her pencil lead scratching across the paper, punctuated by whispered curses and impatient erasures.

By the time he'd finished his sandwich and drained his milk, Lindy still hadn't touched her dinner. He'd extracted everything of interest from the magazine. Bored, he tossed it onto the table and considered Lindy's feet. He'd never really noticed them before. They were actually rather pretty, small and smooth and pink. As she concentrated, she unconsciously bent and flexed her knee, allowing him glimpses of neatly polished, hot pink nails.

His eyes trailed a path upward from her delicate ankles, along her shapely calves, the backs of her knees, her slender, firmly muscled thighs, and finally to her blue-denimed derriere.

He was no longer bored.

Casually, so as not to distract her, he began to massage her left foot. The only indication she gave that he had any effect on her was one quiet sigh, although her pencil scratchings became more erratic the longer he worked.

Feeling devilish, he pressed his lips against her instep, then let his teeth graze the soft flesh there.

She wiggled her toes, but said nothing.

He ran the palm of his hand along her calf. Her skin had the sensual feel of warm satin. He lightly massaged the firm muscle, amazed that she could feel so hard and soft at the same time. His hand inched its way up, past the back of her knee, tracing feather-light trails along her thigh.

He slid quietly off the couch and onto his knees, so he could reach every delectable inch of her. His lips followed the path his hand had taken, nipping and nibbling, tonguing small circles on her skin. He ran his thumb under the ragged edge of her shorts as he found and kissed a sensitive spot near her inner thigh.

Lindy slumped onto her papers, all pretext of homework abandoned. She didn't know whether to be relieved or irritated over Thad's provocative behavior, but after a few more moments of succumbing to the exquisite sensations, she was no longer capable of much in the way of analytical thought.

"Thad Halsey, if you aren't a tempting distraction. Just what do you think you're doing?"

He lifted the hem of her T-shirt and pressed his warm face against the small of her back. "I think I'm seducing you," he answered with unabashed honesty. "I didn't start out with that in mind, but it just sort of... evolved. Did you know you have very sexy feet?"

"I hope you're planning to do this last calculus problem for me. Something tells me I won't finish it."

"I'm a whiz at calculus," he assured her as he deftly maneuvered her onto her back, then kissed her stomach.

"Why did we wait so long?" she asked on a sigh, her voice weakening as a velvet warmth spread from the center-point of her body outward.

"I can't answer for you, but I didn't want to push," he replied, unfastening the metal button on her shorts with loving hands. "You have noticed I sometimes push too hard when I want something, haven't you?"

She had to acknowledge the truth in his words. Still, once they'd crossed a certain line, it had made no sense to her to retreat behind it again.

"You were so reluctant to even see me again," he said as he slowly slid her zipper down. "I just assumed you'd want to... limit things, at least for a while."

"No more limits. I think with us it has to be all or nothing." There was certainly nothing halfway about her response to him, she thought somewhat blearily.

"Lift up, darlin'," he said, tugging on the shorts.

She obeyed, reveling in Thad's appreciative gaze as the cutoffs came free of her hips, revealing a pair of naughty hot-pink panties.

"Good Lord, Lindy, what happened to plain white cotton?" He ran his fingers reverently over the sheer lace, sending shivers coursing in multidirectional tidal waves.

"Pure chance I chose today to wear my birthday present from Twyla," she said with a laugh, followed by a surprised gasp when Thad pressed his mouth against the thin silk covering her feminine mound. She almost panicked when she realized exactly how he intended to make love to her.

She moaned softly, anticipating an intimacy that she knew would bring her so much pleasure as to be almost painful.

He cupped his hand where his mouth had been, his fingers exerting an exquisite pressure. Then he looked up at her, his face flushed with desire, his brown eyes appearing almost black. "What is it, love?"

"The bedroom," she murmured, buying herself a few
more moments of anticipation. She forced herself to sit up,
only then aware that a pencil lead had been jabbing her in
the shoulder, and that her ear had been pressed up against
her calculator. She pulled off her reading glasses and tossed
them onto the couch, then twined her arms around his neck
and kissed him warmly, a gesture of total surrender. She
would make love with him anywhere, any way he wanted,
without question. She'd never extended that degree of trust
to any other man.

With their mouths still locked in a spirited combat, he
lifted her from the sofa. She wound her legs around his
waist, and, with his arms wrapped securely around her hips,
he carried her to her bedroom.

Even as he eased her onto the pale blue eyelet sheets he
never stopped kissing her. Somehow he dispensed with his
clothes and the rest of hers in a fluid way that never left her
wanting for attention, not even for a moment. Once they
were both in a beautifully elemental state, he continued his
gentle assault on her body, kissing and touching every inch
of her from her eyelids to her fingers and toes.

The pleasure was so extraordinary, she had to force herself not to thrash about in sheer delight. Still, she could
withstand his ministrations quietly for only so long; then her
body took its own initiative, responding with a desperate
energy quite apart from her will.

When he kissed her in the most intimate way possible she
was catapulted to a new stage at which pleasure and need
were wound up so tightly together she couldn't tell one from
the other. She heard her own voice crying out, though she
wasn't aware of the exact words. All she knew was that she
wanted fulfillment very badly, and when she got it she'd be
in heaven.

When he pulled away from her she whimpered at the
sudden loss of sensation, but then he was lying beside her,
pulling her against him. Her breasts tingled in a sweet ag-

ony as the crisp hair of his chest abraded her highly aroused
nipples. Then his hand resumed the intimate caress, finding and probing the deliciously sensitive key to her release.

He kissed her ear, a moving, gentle gesture. "You're the
most passionate woman I've ever had the privilege to love,"
he whispered in a voice so sincere it moved Lindy to tears.

She longed to reciprocate, to tell him how he made her
feel beautiful, how he excited her, drove her to levels of
pleasure that exceeded all reason, but she couldn't seem to
formulate the words. Only one level of communication was
left at her disposal, the physical union they both craved. She
parted her legs, resting her knee on his hip, and guided him
gently into her.

He gasped as he entered her, then moaned and sank his
teeth into her shoulder. The slight pain only added to Lindy's sensual overload. She placed her hands on his hips and
pulled him closer, tilting her pelvis to accommodate all of
him.

It was a strangely orchestrated union, with both of them
lying on their sides, but it worked. Together they choreo-
graphed a uniquely timed mating dance, moving in perfect
synchronization, as smoothly as water rippling over stones
in a brook.

She felt the crest coming from a long way off, like a tiny
pinpoint of light in a haze of pleasure, coming closer and
closer until it became the headlamp of a train. When it finally overtook her in a velvety rush, she shook with violent
tremors, crying out Thad's name over and over like a prayer
for deliverance.

They lay in each other's arms for a long time, still save for
the movements of breathing. Lindy became aware of the
ceiling fan overhead and the thin sheen of perspiration that
covered her and now cooled her.

She opened her eyes, finding them moist with tears of the
most powerful emotions she'd ever experienced. She was

both supremely gratified and frightened to death of the intensity Thad had awakened in her.

"Are you with me?" Thad whispered.

She nodded against his shoulder, still not quite able to speak.

"I love how wild you get in my arms, Lindy," he said. "You give me everything...everything. You don't hold one little piece of yourself back. It's the most precious gift anyone's ever given me. I don't want anyone else to ever see you, and feel you, like I do."

The words he spoke smacked dangerously close to commitment. Oddly enough, she didn't object to them, not even silently. The defenses that normally would have sprung forward at the mere hint of permanence were strangely absent.

Feeling unbearably tender toward him, toward the emotions he revealed to her, she stroked his hair and kissed his cheek, and she allowed herself to hope. Just for these few minutes, while they reveled in the exquisite afterglow of lovemaking, she would imagine what it would be like to have Thad as a permanent part of her life. Time enough later, to let reality intrude.

"There is a part of me no one but you will ever see," she said, knowing she'd never spoken truer words. Regardless of what the future brought, even if they went their separate ways, there was a small slice of her soul that was branded with Thad's name, his touch.

They lay in the warm cocoon of afterglow for hours, never quite sleeping but unable to muster the energy to get up. At some point after midnight, however, Thad finally stirred. "I ought to be going, let you get some sleep," he said, kissing her forehead.

Having found such a rare closeness with him, Lindy was loathe to let him go. "I don't need to sleep," she said. "I need you. Please stay with me. I want to wake up in your arms."

He relented without much fuss. "I didn't really want to leave, anyway."

It was early morning, still dark outside, when the phone beside Lindy's bed rang. It awoke Thad first. He was tempted to ignore it, but worried that it might be important at such an ungodly hour, he nudged Lindy awake so she could answer it.

Her hand snaked out from under the pale blue sheet. After a bit of fumbling she located the phone, picked up the receiver and lodged it against her ear. "H'lo? Mm-hmm...Yeah, okay...don't worry about it." She hung up, then sank back into her pillow.

"Lindy? Who was that?"

She sighed and opened her eyes, then smiled like a fallen angel and reached up to touch his stubbly face. "You look gorgeous in the morning," she said, her voice deliciously drowsy. "That was my mother. She has to leave for work in a few minutes, and your truck is blocking her car. Could you move it, please? And hurry back."

Oh, good Lord. Thad felt the blood drain from his face. Judge Shapiro knew he'd spent the night with her daughter.

Once he ruled out blind panic, Thad's first urge was to get angry—at himself, for being so stupid, and at Lindy for tempting him into being so stupid. But he quickly mastered that urge. He couldn't blame this on the beautiful, gloriously naked woman lying next to him in bed.

Nor could he really blame himself. How could a man remain rational when a siren had stolen his wits?

This was just one of those situations, he lectured himself, that he would get into from time to time if he continued to associate with a certain sexy, long-legged blonde. In all fairness, she *had* warned him. He'd accepted the risk, and now he would simply deal with the consequences. Surely she was worth it.

He climbed out of bed and pulled on his clothes, wondering if Judge Shapiro had a violent streak.

Lindy was already back to sleep. He scribbled a quick note in one of her spiral notebooks, ripped out the page and taped it to her pillow in what seemed an appropriately gallant gesture. He hoped she would understand that he couldn't come back to bed. He had to get home, shower, dress, feed Freddy and get to work by a reasonable hour, too.

He left her with a light kiss on the nape of her neck.

As if his situation couldn't get any worse, Marianne Shapiro was exiting the back door of her house just as Thad made his way down Lindy's stairs. He would have preferred to delay a confrontation with her, but he supposed this was better than meeting her in the courtroom.

"Good morning, Thad," she said, her manner disarmingly friendly as she punched the button on an automatic garage door opener, then tucked the device into her briefcase. "I'm sorry I had to wake you, but I do like to get an early start."

"Morning, your honor." Thad's tongue felt three times its normal size. "I . . . I don't know quite what to say," he finally managed, standing with his hand poised on the handle of his truck door. "This is just about the most awkward situation I've ever been in."

"Worse than when Reverend Baumgartner caught you skinny-dipping?"

"A close second," he mumbled.

"Thad," she said, placing a reassuring hand on his arm, "I'm sorry you feel embarrassed, but I promise, I won't break your kneecaps for violating my daughter. Lindy's an adult, capable of making her own decisions. And as for her choice in sleep-over guests, I can't complain. I believe you're a good, decent man. I only have one other thing to say about this, and then we need never speak of it again."

"What's the one thing?" Thad asked, bracing himself.

"I cherish my children above anything in this world, but especially Lindy. She's my ray of sunshine. I have every reason to believe she's in love, probably for the first time in her life. If you hurt her, I'll see you hanged by your eyelashes."

Thad simply stared at Marianne, his mouth hanging open in astonishment.

She smiled pleasantly as she turned toward her car in the garage. "Have a nice day."

Nine

The weather had taken a decidedly nippy turn—appropriate, considering that Halloween was the following week. But the chill wind only compounded the cold brick of pure fear lodged in Thad's chest. He hurried along the sidewalk of a quaint Nacogdoches side street, intent on completing his mission and getting back to work before he could change his mind.

A cheerful jangle of bells greeted him as he entered Emile's, a small custom jeweler's shop. The proprietor, Belva's brother-in-law, greeted Thad with a slightly avaricious smile.

"Belva told me you were coming, Sheriff," the wizened little man said, his words bearing a slight German accent. "I'm sure we can find just the right ring for your special young lady."

Thad cleared his throat and smiled uneasily, grateful to Belva for paving the way for him. He didn't know if he could have voiced his request aloud to a stranger.

It wasn't that he didn't know his own feelings in the matter. He was in love with Lindy—deeply and irrevocably. His life had never been more full or exciting, and he couldn't bear the thought of returning to his boring, pre-Lindy existence. But neither of them had ever made even a passing reference to permanence. As far as he knew, she was still planning to take off for Miami, right after Christmas. She hadn't mentioned it lately, but neither had she expressed any intention of sticking around.

Then why do this now? he asked himself as he studied the bewildering array of rings the jeweler showed him. If he waited another couple of months, he would have time to ease her into the idea. Then by Christmas, their future together would be a foregone conclusion and he could make it official.

But even as that thought crossed his mind, he knew he couldn't put it off another two months.

Ever since the night he'd so wrongly accused her of not having a reputation to protect, he had become acutely sensitive to just how other people saw Lindy. He'd discovered that while everyone thought she was outrageous and flamboyant, her moral character was never at issue. In fact, now that the whole damn county knew he and Lindy were sleeping together, many people had adopted a protective attitude toward her, as if they had to defend her against his fast, big-city ways.

More than one indignant person had asked Thad, point blank, when he planned to "make an honest woman of Lindy." And then there was Kevin, whose sly remarks about his own sister had almost earned him a black eye, and Judge Shapiro, who every so often treated him to a threatening lift of one eyebrow that said more than any words could.

He *had* to ask Lindy, even if he was rushing a bit, and he had to do it in such a way that she couldn't turn him down. The answer, he'd decided in a flash of brilliance last night, was to dazzle her thoroughly with flowers, dinner, dancing, a ring and a sincere request, made from one knee. She would be so impressed with the grandness of his financial and emotional risk that she couldn't say no.

Emile expounded on the merits of one stone's cut, another's clarity, the clever setting of a third, but Thad hardly heard. He was overwhelmed by the enormity of what he was about to do.

"These are all nice—really nice," he finally said, not wishing to insult the jeweler's fine work, "but I'm looking for something more... unusual. Maybe something with a little color?"

Emile whisked away the tray of diamond solitaires. "Of course, of course. Such provincial rings are no match for your lady's uniqueness, yes?"

"Yes," Thad agreed, gratified that Emile saw the problem so clearly.

"I have in the back a special ring. Let me get it." He returned a moment later with a handful of royal blue velvet. He spread it onto the glass counter and gently laid his prize on top of it.

The moment Thad saw the ring, he knew it was the right one—a stone of the purest, deepest green he'd ever seen, cut into a perfect square. The stone was flanked by two small, rectangular diamonds, and all of it was mounted on a thick gold band. It managed to look substantial yet not at all clumsy. He could already see it gracing Lindy's long, slender finger.

"It's an emerald," Emile said in a hushed, reverent tone. "It's not so large, but it is one of the finest stones I've ever had the pleasure to cut."

"I'll take it."

Emile's eyes widened, obviously surprised at the swiftness of Thad's decision. "But sir, we haven't even discussed the price...."

"I don't care." He'd just given the man an engraved invitation to gouge him, he realized, and he still didn't care.

A few months ago, he never would have purchased anything based on emotion. He would have shopped for weeks, comparing and contrasting, weighing his options, taking his budget into consideration. He was not the same man he'd been, and he was glad.

How sad that she didn't even own a real dress, Lindy thought with a scowl as she slipped a borrowed one over her head. Thankfully her mother had a whole closet full of cocktail dresses, suitable for a fancy dinner in Shreveport, which was where she and Thad were headed this evening.

He'd asked her more than a week ago for this date. And because he'd pointed out that in all the weeks they'd been seeing each other, they had never once given themselves a special, dress-up evening, she'd agreed. Somehow she'd get her schoolwork done, even if she had to stay up all night.

Once she got the dress zipped she went into the bathroom and climbed onto the edge of her tub, attempting to see all of herself in the wavy glass over the sink. She desperately needed a full-length mirror. She remembered seeing a pretty cherry-wood mirror in Andersen's Antiques that would look great in her bedroom. Maybe she could—

She closed her eyes and put a hand to her forehead as she hopped off the bathtub. That was the second time today she'd caught a thought like that sneaking into her consciousness—thoughts that implied she planned to stay here indefinitely. She'd never before been tempted to acquire any possessions that wouldn't fit in the trunk of her car.

Watch yourself, Lindy, an inner voice warned her. She and Thad had been seeing each other for over three months now—a record in the relationship department for both of them. It couldn't last much longer, could it? With a groan, she acknowledged that she desperately wanted it to last. She'd never been happier than she had these last few weeks.

Even her calculus class, a persistent thorn in her side, had taken on new and exciting significance. For once in her life, she was facing a difficult challenge head on and sticking with it even when things didn't go her way. Her dogged persistence had surprised everyone, but especially her. Somewhere in the back of her mind was an insidiously tempting little thought: *If you can defeat calculus, Lindy, then you can do anything you put your mind to.*

"Anything" included forming a lifelong attachment to one man. But she didn't allow herself to dwell long on that possibility. She wasn't at all sure she could do it, and until she *was* sure, she refused to even toy with the idea.

Someone knocked at her door. It was much too early to be Thad.

"Coming," she called out as she walked toward the door in her stockinged feet. As she passed through the living room, her calculus notebook caught her eye from its perch on the sofa. Peeking from its cover was the edge of her midterm exam. Her instructor had passed out copies of the test, along with the answers, as each student had exited the classroom, so they could determine what grade they would receive. Lindy, shrinking from the possibly unpleasant truth, had yet to check her answers.

She opened the door to find her mother standing outside. "I brought your mail," she said, handing Lindy a bundle of letters and a magazine. "You haven't picked it up for a couple of days. And I found some earrings and a necklace that go perfectly with that dress...is something wrong, sweetheart?"

Lindy's eyes were transfixed on a slick, computer-generated envelope in her hand. "My midterm grades," she said, her throat suddenly dry.

"Oh. Why don't you look at them?"

She turned away from her mother and, with very deliberate motions, set the bundle of mail on the coffee table. "I'm afraid to look."

"Why? You've been working so hard, I'm sure they're fine. You've always made excellent grades. Anyway, is it that important? You told me you were taking those classes for the sake of mental stimulation."

You have no idea how important, Lindy thought. She needed a near-perfect grade point average if she wanted to get into vet school. "You're right, it doesn't really matter," she hedged.

Marianne looked unconvinced. "Do you want me to peek?"

"No! Um, no," she said again, trying to adopt a carefree demeanor. "I just don't want to think about school tonight. Let's see those earrings."

The dainty diamond earrings and matching necklace accented the low-cut black dress perfectly. Lindy thanked her mother profusely for the fashion advice, then rushed her out the door. She needed some time alone before Thad arrived, some time to regroup, get her jangled nerves under control.

She tried to distract herself by keeping busy. She filed and polished her nails, applied her makeup with infinite care, experimented with several different shades of lipstick. But never could she completely banish the image of the envelope sitting on her coffee table.

She would have to look. If she didn't, she'd be a nervous wreck all through dinner and the evening would be ruined.

With measured, slow paces she walked to the living room, picked up the envelope, clenched her eyes shut and peeled it open. For several seconds she simply held it to her chest without looking, issuing a silent, fervent prayer. Then she opened her eyes.

Thad knew something was wrong the moment Lindy opened her door. There was nothing outwardly amiss. In fact, she looked even more breathtaking than usual. Her normally uncontrollable curls had been tamed into an elegant upsweep. Diamonds sparkled at her ears and around her slender neck. The simple black dress she wore clung

provocatively to her curves, revealing just enough of the
gentle swell of her breasts to make him want to see more.

But it was her eyes that told the story—huge and bright
and undeniably sad.

At her invitation he came inside, handing her a large white
florist's box—step one of his campaign to convince her to
marry him.

"You didn't have to—" she started to say, but he inter-
rupted her.

"I wanted to."

She opened the box with trembling hands. When she
folded back the tissue paper to reveal the one dozen long-
stem red roses, she exploded into tears.

He'd never seen her cry so much, and the sight unnerved
him—especially because these were not tears of joy. He took
the flowers out of her limp hands and set them down, then
folded her into his arms, tamping down his own alarm.
"Lindy, honey, what is it?"

She fought her way out of his embrace and turned her
back on him. After a few moments she got the sobs under
control. "It's nothing, really," she said as she found a box
of tissue and dabbed at her eyes. "I just received a dose of
reality and I'm not handling it with much dignity." She
nodded toward a scrap of paper resting on the arm of the
sofa.

Thad picked up the paper, stared at it for a few seconds,
then understood all too well. Stat—A. Chem—A. Calc…D.

Lindy had just run smack into a brick wall, and she didn't
have a clue as to how to deal with it.

"It's only midterm," he said, wanting so badly to take
that tragic, lost look out of her eyes. "There's still time to
bring up your grade."

But she was shaking her head. "It's no use. I'll never
catch on to calculus. I probably just wasn't meant to get a
degree—" She cut herself off.

"So that's what you had in mind." He'd known all along there was some reason for her odd selection of classes. "What sort of degree are you working toward?" he asked cautiously.

She shrugged. "It's not important. I'm going over to the university tomorrow and withdraw."

Thad fought the panic welling up inside him. He didn't know how or why, but her success or failure with this stupid calculus class was somehow tied to him, to their relationship. If she gave up on school, she might be tempted to give up on a lot of things—including him.

He had to force himself not to overreact. She was upset right now, he reasoned; that was all. As soon as she'd had some time to think about it, she'd realize she had other options besides simply quitting.

"You look like you could use a steak dinner," he said, touching her arm. "Let's go out, have a nice evening together, maybe do some dancing, and forget all about your grades for a while. I'm sure you'll feel a lot better—"

"Could we do it another time? I'm not very good company tonight."

"You don't have to be. I plan to be so fascinating, so vastly entertaining, you won't have to..."

But again she shook her head.

He ought to let it go. He knew that; but he also knew that if he didn't carry through with his plans tonight, he might lose his nerve. "Lindy, we've been planning this evening for a long time," he argued.

"I know, but it would be wasted on me. Can't you change the dinner reservations to another night?"

"No! I mean, it has to be tonight."

She stared at him, bewildered. "Why?"

"Because, dammit, I have something very special planned."

"What?"

He ran an impatient hand through his hair. Things were not progressing in a promising manner. "All right, have it your way. But bear in mind, this would have been a lot more romantic if we were sitting at a corner table at Andre's, sipping champagne." Now that he was committed to the decision, he was anxious to get it over with. He reached inside the breast pocket of his jacket, extracted a silver velvet box, and handed it to her.

Her hands trembled violently as she eased open the lid. She gasped. "My God, Thad, it's...beautiful. But why?"

"Because I love you." The declaration had been surprisingly easy—perhaps because he'd been living with the knowledge of his love for a long time, even if he hadn't admitted it until recently. "I know an emerald isn't a conventional stone for an engagement ring—"

"Engagement ring?" All the color drained from her face. "Are you crazy?"

The harshness of the question put him off, but only for a moment. "Probably. You've brought nothing but trouble into my life, but you know what? I'm starting to *like* trouble."

His admission produced not even the ghost of a smile on Lindy's face.

"How about it, Lindy? Marry me?"

She snapped the box closed and thrust it back into his hands. "I can't marry you," she said, her words all but strangled with emotion.

He was prepared for this. He'd known she might not be an easy sell. "Why not?"

"Oh, Thad, don't you see? How could I possibly hope to conquer something as long-term as marriage when I can't even succeed at getting a college degree?"

"Can't succeed, or won't?"

"Can't!" she insisted. "I've worked my tail off for the past eight weeks. Doesn't that D say it all?"

"You can graduate with Ds. Besides, I also see two As on your report card. Don't those count for anything?"

"Not enough," she said softly, her eyes staring off at some invisible point in the distance.

"So you won't marry me because you're having a little trouble with calculus?"

"I can't marry you because I don't see how it can last."

He failed to see the connection. "Tell me, what relationship comes with guarantees?"

She wouldn't answer him.

"What ever happened to the joy of taking risks, hmm? You're the one who taught me to take chances, for crissakes. Now that I'm willing to stick my neck out, you're hiding in your shell. Does that make sense?" As his voice increased in volume, he realized he was dangerously close to losing his temper.

"This isn't getting us anywhere," she finally said. "Maybe you'd better go."

"We have to talk about this, Lindy."

"There's nothing to talk about. My mind's made up."

"Well, fine. That's just fine," he said, heading for the door. "If we can't even discuss something as important as this, then we don't have much of a relationship. Adios, Lindy." He banged the door shut behind him but got no satisfaction at all from the effort.

Lindy stared at the closed door. There was something terrifyingly final about the way he'd slammed it, about the way he'd said goodbye.

When she realized she'd been holding a deep breath, she expelled it slowly. Well, she'd known this would happen sooner or later. Her relationship with Thad had been primed for an explosion. It had lasted just a little over three months. She should be grateful for the brief time they'd had together.

But she didn't feel at all grateful. Instead, she felt small and mean-spirited. Absently she extracted one of the roses from the box and brushed the soft petals against her cheek. Thad loved her. He loved her enough to marry her, and she'd reacted by hurting him. She'd once warned him this might happen, but that was no consolation.

She paced the small apartment, replaying the hurtful scene in her mind. Could she have said something, done something, differently? she wondered with a gnawing frustration inside her. But no matter how she played it, she always arrived at the same unavoidable conclusion. There would be no happily ever after for herself and Thad.

After a few more moments of deliberation, she decided on a course of action that would be best for everyone involved.

Thad left his suit in a crumpled heap on the floor, opting instead for his softest, most faded pair of jeans and a well-washed flannel shirt.

Food came next—comfort food, to go with comfort clothes. He would make chili. Perfect.

On his way through the living room he spied Freddy peering mournfully through the glass door. She was almost six months old now, with the size and appetite of a small horse. With an uncanny respect for Thad's state of mind, she didn't bound through the door when he opened it, as was her usual habit, but padded in quietly and thrust her big head into his hand for a mandatory scratch behind the ears.

He dropped to one knee and wrapped his arms around her muscular neck, pressing his face against the soft, black fur. She wagged her tail and licked his ear with unconditional affection.

Why couldn't human relationships be that straightforward? he wondered as he threw two pounds of shredded beef into a skillet. Why couldn't Lindy simply accept his love, or acknowledge her own love for him? Why did she have to tie their relationship into a straitjacket of conditions to be met and tests to be passed?

Of all the people in the world, he'd never have guessed Lindy could let fear rule her life. He'd once thought she led a charmed existence, that fate simply handed to her on a silver platter whatever she wanted or needed. He'd been wrong.

With a blinding flash of insight, he saw her for what she really was. She wasn't charmed, or even lucky. She was a quitter. Sure, a lot of things came easily for her. But anything that didn't, she abandoned immediately so that she didn't risk failure. Lindy Shapiro, who preached to him so eloquently about the joys of taking risks, had never risked anything really important.

He transferred the beef to his slow cooker and added a selection of spices, not bothering to measure them. As he chopped up an onion, he was suddenly anxious to talk to her again. He shouldn't have left her. He should have been more patient in the face of her emotional outburst.

He would go back, that's what he'd do, he decided as he dumped a can of pureed tomatoes into his spicy concoction. He would sit her down and make her see that she was sabotaging her own happiness with this defeatist attitude. Who would tell her if he didn't? Who would ever love her the way he did, love her enough to be tough on her?

Once the chili ingredients were mixed, he turned the slow cooker on low. Hell, he'd wanted something to eat *now*. Why had he started a pot of food that wouldn't be ready until tomorrow?

He was too tired to cook something else. He'd drive over to the Happy Camper diner in Corrigan and get the biggest chicken-fried steak the cook could scare up. But even as he shoved his arms into the sleeves of his denim jacket, he knew he was just making an excuse so he could get back into his truck and head toward Lindy's.

By the time he pulled into her driveway he had a whole new arsenal of persuasive tactics to use on her. He actually felt optimistic—until he drove around to the back and realized her car was gone. Now where had she run off to?

He would wait for her. She had to come home, sooner or later.

He parked, climbed the steps two at a time, and unlocked her door with the key she'd given him. All was dark and quiet. He fumbled for the light switch, found it, flipped it on.

What he saw put his senses on red alert, but only for a moment. At first glance it appeared as if a burglar had tossed the place, it was such a mess. Upon closer inspection, however, the true state of affairs became obvious: Lindy, in too much of a hurry to do it neatly, had packed up her belongings and vacated. She was gone, lock, stock and Cadillac.

"Dammit!" he said aloud, kicking a half-packed box of books that she'd apparently decided to leave behind. He should have seen this coming. But there wasn't time for self-recriminations. He had to figure out where she'd gone and figure it out fast. She could have as much as an hour on him.

He took a fast tour of her apartment, looking for clues, and found one. On a pad of paper by the bedroom phone was written a number, area code 305. Miami, if his memory served him correctly.

"Lindy, you're only making this hard on yourself," he murmured as he tore the page off and stuck it in his pocket. He was furious with her. How could she walk out without even saying goodbye? Hell, how could she walk out, period? But he'd deal with the anger later. Right now, he had to find her, and for that he needed his coldest, most calculating professional instincts. Time enough to let his temper fly when he caught up with her.

But he wasn't going to lose his temper, he reminded himself, not unless he intended to drive her away for good. No, he had something else in mind for this runaway.

The last thing he did before leaving her apartment was to gather up her books and papers. As he set them on the bucket seat next to him, he made a decision. He would have to drive all the way to Winstonia to get a squad car before he could go after Lindy. The delay would lengthen her head start, but he needed his two-way radio—not to mention the lights and siren.

Midnight had come and gone. As Lindy approached the Louisiana-Mississippi border, she realized she hadn't eaten since lunch. Maybe she should find a motel and stop for the night. But the impulse to keep moving was strong. Even if she did stop, she wouldn't be able to sleep. As long as she kept her brain occupied with the road ahead of her, and with the inane chatter from the radio, she didn't have to think about what she was doing. But left idle, her mind would return to that scene in her apartment.

Still, if she planned to drive all night, she needed to eat. Seeing a garish sign for a truck stop up ahead, she took the next exit.

She pulled the Cadillac into a parking spot and cut the engine. Before opening the door, she paused to finger the soft petals of her roses, nestled in green tissue paper on the seat next to her. She'd taken very little with her, figuring she wouldn't need much as a maid on a cruise ship. But she hadn't been able to part with the flowers—even if they did serve as a hurtful reminder of the love she'd left behind.

They were already wilting. Maybe she shouldn't have brought them. Then she could have remembered them as they'd looked when she first opened the box—fresh and vibrant. Now she'd have to watch them slowly die.

"Halsey, you there?"

Thad reached for the radio handset. "I'm here. Any news?" In a highly irregular request, he had asked for the cooperation of the Louisiana highway patrol in locating

Lindy. He'd been completely honest with them. Over the
two-way radio, he'd explained that he was a Texas county
sheriff, and that he was trying to catch up with the woman
he loved so he could convince her to marry him.

Eager to help out a fellow lawman in trouble, every patrolman working Interstate-20 had promised to be on the
unofficial lookout for the red Cadillac.

"I've located your quarry, Sheriff," came the answer.
"There's a car with Texas plates matching the description,
parked at the Four Corners Truck Stop. It's five miles west
of the state line. I think your lady friend must be inside getting a bite to eat. Want me to detain her? Looks like she
might have a broken taillight."

"Just keep an eye on her," Thad answered. He figured he
was maybe ten miles away. With a rush of adrenaline
brought on by the prospect of catching up with his prey, he
pressed down on the accelerator.

He had the truck stop's sign in view when the anony-
mous patrolman's voice came back over the radio. "She's
leaving the parking lot," he reported. "Looks like she's
heading...east. Yep, she's getting back on the interstate
toward Mississippi."

"I'm right behind her," Thad said. He passed the exit,
then slowed as he approached the entrance ramp. Sure
enough, Lindy's red car appeared. He pulled into the lane
in back of it.

Lindy's heart raced in automatic panic when she saw the
lights flashing in her mirror. She looked down at her speedometer, relieved to see that she definitely had not been
speeding. Was the cop after someone else?

No, she decided when he sounded one angry blip with his
siren. Resignedly she pulled onto the shoulder. It was probably the broken taillight. The highway patrol must be bored
tonight.

She opened her window, deciding she didn't have the energy to try to get out of a ticket. She'd just accept it and move on.

"Evenin' ma'am. Mind stepping out of the car?"

Oh, no. It couldn't be. But it was. There was no mistaking that voice. She rested her head in her arms against the steering wheel. "Thad, what are you doing here?" she asked without looking up.

"I'm stopping you from doing something you'll regret the rest of your life," he answered. She could hear the cold fury behind his words, and a frisson of uneasiness worked its way up her spine. She was in trouble—big trouble.

A second car, lights flashing, pulled up behind Thad's Scanlon County squad car. Another police vehicle, coming from the opposite direction, slowed down, then turned on his lights and sped up.

"Good heavens, Thad, what did you do, call in a SWAT team?"

He didn't reply. Instead, he opened her door for her. "Just get your purse and step out of the car. You're coming with me."

"Like hell! Who do you think you are, Thad Halsey? You can't just order me to go with you. And you can't arrest me, either. Even if you had a reason, *which* you don't, you're out of your jurisdiction." She slammed the door shut again.

"I wasn't planning to arrest you," he said in a deceptively cordial tone. "Not if I don't have to."

By now the other police car had stopped. Three sets of flashing lights paused on the shoulder of the highway were creating a spectacle. More than one passerby had slowed down to take a look.

The other two lawmen stepped out of their cars and approached Thad. Lindy watched with undisguised interest, expecting them to give him the third degree about the fact that he was in Louisiana, not Texas. But to her dismay they both introduced themselves and shook hands with him, grinning broadly.

"Well, now," the taller of the two said, eyeing her car speculatively. "Let's have a look at her."

She'd had about all of this she could take. She'd let them have a look at her, all right, but they'd have to listen to her, too. She opened the door and swung out of the car, giving Thad a look cold enough to freeze his gizzard before turning her gaze on the other two men.

The tall patrolman whistled through his teeth in wordless approval, which only incensed Lindy further. She would have liked to tell them they were all redneck chauvinist pigs, but seeing as she was outnumbered and out-machoed, she decided a little more subtlety was needed.

"Excuse me," she said as she folded her arms and leaned her hips against the side of her car, "but can any of you give me even a vague reason as to why I was pulled over?"

The other two looked to Thad for an answer.

"You didn't leave me any choice," he said. "What was I supposed to do, just stand by and let you run out of my life?"

Lindy glanced nervously at the other two men. "Do we have to discuss this in front of an audience?"

"Not if you'll come back home with me."

She shook her head adamantly. "I've made my decision. It's best for both of us. I wasn't meant to settle down—can't you see that?"

"No, I can't see it, not at all."

"Well, I don't know how to make it any clearer. And unless you're going to arrest me, I'll assume I'm free to go. Right, gentlemen?" She looked at the two patrolmen. "I know how to kick up a pretty big fuss when it comes to the violation of my civil rights."

They glanced uneasily at each other, and then at Thad. "She's right," one of them said.

Thad squared his shoulders and stepped directly into Lindy's path as she tried to get back into the car. "Lindy, I didn't want to have to resort to this, but you're...you're a chicken."

"A *what?*"

"A chicken! A coward. A lily-livered wuss. You're all talk and no action. All that stuff about taking risks was a bunch of bull hockey. You wouldn't know how to deal with a real challenge if it bit you on the butt."

"Thad, what has gotten *into* you?" She tried to step around him but he anticipated her, blocking her path once again.

"You're afraid, Lindy. You met with one little setback and you're doing what you always do—running away. Why don't you grow up and face your problems?"

She could almost feel the steam coming out of her ears. "How dare you?" She had to clasp her hands together tightly to keep herself from striking out at him.

"Go ahead, slap me. Isn't that what you want to do?"

"Thad Halsey, I promised myself I'd never slap you again and I won't. But I swear, if you don't get out of my way..."

"What'll you do? Tell your mother? That's how spoiled little rich girls like you deal with their problems, isn't it?"

"I'm warning you, Thad...."

"Spoiled brat," he taunted.

She'd sworn she wouldn't slap him, but she'd never said anything about kicking. She struck swiftly with the heel of her cowboy boot.

Thad groaned and clutched his left shin to a chorus of laughter from the peanut gallery.

"Way to go, Lindy," one of the patrolmen said. "I'd say he had that one coming."

The other one scratched his chin thoughtfully. "I think he's got the upper hand now, though."

"Oh, go away, won't you?" she said sharply. Then all the fight simply drained out of her. She turned back to Thad. "I'm sorry."

"Not half as sorry as I am," he said wryly, wincing as he rubbed the injury. But then a smile spread slowly across his face—not an altogether pleasant smile, either. "Guess what, Lindy?" he asked as he straightened. "You just assaulted an officer. You're under arrest."

Ten

"**Y**ou did that on purpose!" Lindy protested as Thad escorted her to his squad car with an insistent hand at her elbow.

"Of course I did," he replied evenly. "Of all the times for you to be slow to provoke—I was about to run out of insults."

She made one final appeal to the other two officers. "He can't do this, can he? He's out of his jurisdiction!"

"He can if we let him," the taller officer answered.

"And frankly, we'd just as soon let him take you back to your own state," said the other one as he chuckled and elbowed his friend in the ribs. "The Louisiana legal system isn't ready for you."

With a sigh of exasperation she climbed into the back seat. She awarded Thad a lethal look just before he closed the door, but her efforts seemed to be lost on him. So was the silent treatment she gave him as he pulled the car onto the interstate. His personal brick wall was firmly in place.

Five minutes of dead quiet was about all she could take. "Am I really under arrest?" she finally asked, leaning forward and speaking through the wire mesh that separated back from front seat.

"Yes."

"What about my car?"

"Don't worry, I'll send someone for it."

"You could get in a lot of trouble, you know. You absconded out of state with a county vehicle. You used your position and your authority for personal reasons. You're not even in uniform."

"Bring it up at the arraignment."

"When's that?"

"Tomorrow. Maybe. We'll have to call in another judge. I don't think your mother could be impartial."

"I suppose you'll throw me in jail until then?"

His lack of response was downright scary.

"Look, can we talk about this? I know you're angry with me—"

"'Angry' doesn't begin to describe it, lady. You've had your chance to talk, and you chose instead to run off to Florida. We'll talk when I'm good and ready."

And knowing you, not a moment sooner, she added silently as she pulled off her boots. It was more than three hours back to Winstonia. She had a feeling it might be the longest three hours of her life.

Her body felt every mile she'd traveled over the past few hours. Suddenly she was exhausted. She stretched out on the seat and pulled her knees into her chest, and soon the gentle thump-thump of tires on pavement lulled her into an untroubled sleep.

It was after four in the morning by the time Thad woke her up with a rough announcement that they'd arrived at the courthouse. He stood by impatiently, with the car door hanging open, as she pulled on her boots. The cold, early-morning air revived her as he escorted her inside.

In the sheriff's office, Jimmy McGruder was covering the graveyard shift on dispatch. He sat up quickly and pulled his feet off Belva's desk when the door opened, attempting to hide the science-fiction paperback he'd been reading. "What are you doing here this time of night, Sheriff?" he asked sheepishly.

"Got a prisoner for you," Thad replied, nodding toward Lindy. "You can start typing her arrest papers."

Jimmy just stared, his mouth hanging open.

"Don't I get a phone call?" Lindy asked.

Thad shrugged, reached into his jeans pocket and pulled out a quarter. "Here you go," he said as he flipped it to her. "You know where the pay phone is."

As she dialed her mother's number, she remembered the last time she'd used this phone. A lot had changed in four months—and yet here she was, in trouble with the law again. It was almost funny—but not quite.

Marianne answered the phone in a sleepy grumble. As soon as she heard Lindy's voice, however, she became suddenly alert. "Lindy, good grief, where are you?"

"In jail. Thad arrested me."

Marianne groaned. "Dare I ask what happened? The abbreviated version, please."

"Well, I was almost to the Mississippi border when—"

"What? You mean you ran off without telling him? Without telling *me*?"

"I was going to call you . . ."

"Lindy, you're my daughter and I love you, but sometimes I think you belong behind bars. Call me back at a civilized hour, and *maybe* I'll bail you out." *Click*.

Lindy hung up, defeated. She was too tired to fight this any longer. She would spend the night in jail—what the hell? There were worse things, although when she saw the holding cell she almost changed her mind.

"This is disgusting!" she said as she sank gingerly onto the lumpy cot and surveyed the barren cell. Its only concession to personal comfort was a sink and a stool behind a movable screen. She felt the first stirrings of true despair. "Are you really going to leave me here?"

She thought she saw the slightest softening around the hard lines of Thad's mouth, and then a moment of indecision playing about his features. To her surprise he stepped into the cell with her and closed the door behind him.

"Okay," he said as he pulled a wooden chair close to where she perched on the edge of the cot, "let's cut the crap. I didn't arrest you just for the sake of tormenting you." He sank into the chair and leaned forward, resting his elbows on his knees. "I'm still madder than hell at you, and I don't imagine you're all that thrilled with me. But I'm going to push that aside for now. Can you do the same?"

Ordinarily she would have refused to back down. But suddenly his velvety brown eyes looked so sincere that she found herself nodding slowly in agreement.

"Good. Now, then, I'll make a deal with you. It's about four-thirty. If you'll cooperate with me for the next three hours—till seven-thirty—I'll forget the arrest and you can go."

"Cooperate how?" she wanted to know.

"I'm going to tutor you in calculus."

"*What?*" The man was out of his gourd. Jail was preferable to three hours of calculus—well, maybe not quite. She shrugged. "If that's what it takes. What do you know about calculus?"

"Enough. Wait here."

He disappeared, leaving the jail cell door open. She toyed briefly with the idea of escape, but she didn't relish the thought of becoming a fugitive.

He came back a few minutes later with a pile of books under his arm—*her* books, she realized. "What are you doing with those?"

"Never mind. Scoot over."

She did. To her utter amazement, he sat next to her on the cot and proceeded to do exactly as he'd threatened. He tutored her. She took the blank midterm exam her professor had given out and reworked the problems exactly as she had during the real test, explaining her steps to Thad as she went. He stopped her whenever she made a false move, gently pointing out how she'd gone wrong.

Morning sunlight slanted through the cell's barred window by the time they'd finished. Lindy was exhausted—but she also had a glimmer of understanding about the subject matter that she'd lacked before. "How come my teacher doesn't explain it the way you do?" she asked through a yawn.

"Because he's not as motivated as I am. He doesn't care whether you learn it or not. I do."

"That's nice." She closed her eyes and took a deep breath. "Can I go home now?"

"Not quite. I have till seven-thirty, remember?"

She grimaced. "You're not going to make me work out any more problems, are you?"

"No. All I want is a few honest answers from you. Then you can leave."

"I suppose you deserve at least that," she conceded as she again pulled off her boots, then curled her legs under her and leaned against the cinderblock wall. "What do you want to know?"

Apparently he'd been thinking through exactly what he wanted to ask, because he didn't hesitate a heartbeat. "What kind of degree are you working toward?"

She took a deep breath and sat up a little straighter. She hadn't admitted this aloud to anyone except Dottie Wang, who'd been sworn to secrecy. "Preveterinary medicine. I was planning to get some of the basics out of the way at Stephen F., then transfer to Texas A & M next fall."

"And why was it so important to get a good grade in calculus?"

"I have to get good grades in *everything*," she said as a familiar sense of hopelessness overwhelmed her again. "It's hard to get into vet school—harder even than medical school. I'm competing with fresh, bright, energetic kids who make straight As. I could get away with one or two Bs, but a *D*? No way."

"And that's why you want to quit? Because you're afraid to put in a lot of work and then have your application to vet school denied?"

"I'm quitting school because I don't have a prayer," she corrected him. "This happened to me in my first semester in college, too. I enrolled in the prevet program at A & M, and at midterm I was failing calculus." She swallowed hard, trying to get rid of the lump that had started growing in the back of her throat. "My adviser recommended that I change to a less demanding major."

"So you let some idiot adviser talk you out of the career you wanted," Thad concluded. "He didn't suggest any other alternatives? Like tutoring?"

She shook her head as a traitorous tear escaped her eye. "I figured I'd set my sights too high, and I tried to find something else that I wanted to be, but I never did." The words came out in a rush, right along with a whole lot of tears. Why did she suddenly hurt so much?

For those few moments, Thad felt her pain as deeply as if it were his own. He understood her now, perhaps better than she did herself. More than anything, he wanted to hold her, comfort her, but he knew there was something much more important he could do for her right now. He could give her back her dream.

"So what's stopping you from getting what you want?"

She stared at him, blinked a couple of times. "Haven't you been listening? My calculus grade—"

"So one stupid class, one stupid grade, is going to hold you back?"

"It has so far," she mumbled, wiping her eyes with the back of her hand.

Thad handed her a handkerchief, which she accepted with a sniff of gratitude. "If you could bring your grade up to, say, a B by the end of the semester," he queried, "would that be good enough?"

"But there's no way—"

"Just answer the question," he admonished softly.

"A B would be heaven."

"With my help, you can do it," he stated confidently. "So, now we have that problem out of the way. Let's talk about why a little marriage proposal scared you out of your skin."

She peered at him from beneath her lashes for a few moments, unsure whether she wanted to accept the abrupt change of subject. "Your timing could have been better," she finally said. "You didn't catch me in the most receptive state of mind. Not only that, but you surprised me. I had no idea you were planning to spring something like that on me."

"I know I jumped the gun," he conceded.

"Why?" she wanted to know.

He rolled his eyes. "Everyone from the mayor to your mother thinks I've compromised your virtue. If there's not a wedding pretty soon, they'll ride me out of town on a rail."

Lindy was amazed that she could laugh. "What nerve! If I don't worry about my virtue, why should they?"

"Then there's Kevin and Twyla, announcing their engagement. Makes us look a little slow, know what I mean?"

Lindy sobered. "Did you propose to me just to ease your conscience? So you could say that you asked, and I turned you down?"

He shook his head. "Sorry, but that's not the case. I would marry you tomorrow if you'd agree. And you did turn me down, remember? I wasn't too thrilled."

"Oh, yeah." She toyed with the frayed hem of her jeans.

"One more question," he said. "Do you love me?"

She wished to hell she could lie about it. It would be so much simpler. "Yes, I love you."

"But you don't want to marry me, right?"

Again, nothing but the truth would work this time. "I'd give anything to marry you, but... it's a lifetime commitment, and, as I'm sure you've noticed, I have trouble with any commitment longer than an hour or two. I don't want us to end up hurting each other."

Some of his carefully banked anger smoldered to the surface. "Nothing could hurt more than having you walk out without a word."

"You're the one who said we didn't have a relationship," she pointed out, matching his anger heated word for heated word. "You're the one who said 'adios' and slammed the door."

"I didn't mean it."

"And I didn't mean to walk out. It just happened. Anyway, I would have come back," she added lamely.

"All right, so we both say and do stupid things. Does that mean we should give up on it?"

"I don't know... no, I guess we shouldn't just throw it away, but I'm so afraid..." She couldn't quite bring herself to voice her fears.

"Afraid of what?" he asked, so suddenly gentle it took her breath away.

When she answered him, she said the words very slowly, very distinctly. "I'm afraid that I'm incapable of seeing anything through till the end, including a marriage. If I could just once prove to myself that I can finish something—"

"Like calculus?"

She saw a spark in his gaze that alarmed her. She'd unwittingly given him a challenge. "Your time's almost up," she said, glancing nervously at her watch.

Her warning didn't faze him. "Lindy, I'm telling you that you can have whatever you want if you're willing to work for it, including a B in calculus. I can help you do it."

She shook her head. "That's not possible. I have to make perfect scores on all the tests and the final—"

"It *is* possible. If you want it bad enough."

Suddenly she did. She could almost taste that B.

"I'll make another deal with you," he said, as if he sensed her softening. "If you let me work with you, and you try real hard, and you still can't bring your grade up to a B, then you can take off for Miami or Mexico or whatever, and I won't lift a finger to stop you. No scenes, no arguments."

"And if I do make the grade?" she asked, though she was pretty sure she knew the answer.

"You marry me."

Thad was chopping up the ingredients for beef stew one December evening when Lindy breezed into his kitchen, looking like a brightly wrapped holiday package. She had on a vivid green, oversized sweater, black knit pants and a red velvet ribbon in her hair. It was all Thad could do to resist unwrapping her.

"I didn't hear you come in," he said before he gave her a chaste kiss on one rosy cheek.

"Freddy didn't announce me the way she usually does. Where is she?"

"Banished to the outdoors. Did you see what she did to my Christmas tree?"

Lindy went to the doorway and peered into the living room, then laughed out loud. "It's a good thing that dog didn't grow any taller, or you wouldn't have any needles on the *top* half of your tree, either. At least she didn't bother the packages."

"Just one. Gilbert Foster gave me one of those gift baskets—you know, with meats and cheeses?"

Lindy nodded, trying and failing to suppress a smile.

"Freddy ate the beef stick, wrapper and all, and had started on the summer sausage by the time I caught her."

Lindy clamped a hand over her mouth, but the chuckles escaped anyway. "I'm sorry... I know this is one of those occasions when I'm not supposed to laugh, but..."

"Go ahead, laugh," he told her, subtly brandishing his meat cleaver. "You'll get yours later."

"Sounds like you have a tough lesson in store for me tonight," she grumbled. "You're a cruel taskmaster, Thad Halsey. Cruel and unreasonable." She stole a carrot from his cutting board and crunched down on it.

"What did you make on your last test?" He knew the score as well as she did. She'd practically had it tattooed onto her forehead, she'd been so ecstatic.

"Ninety-seven," she answered dutifully.

"That's right," he said smugly. "I might be cruel and unreasonable, but I get the job done. Besides, I do give you a little reward now and then, don't I?"

That made her smile wickedly. She came up behind him and wrapped her arms around his rib cage, pressing her warmth against his back. "Those rewards are too few and far between. For the past seven weeks I've been eating, drinking, breathing and dreaming calculus, with far too little recreation to break up the monotony."

He agreed with her. Lindy spent every waking moment with her nose in a textbook. When she wasn't studying, she was working or sleeping.

Only once in the past few weeks had they put aside the books and indulged in an evening strictly for play—the night Lindy came home with her almost-perfect test score. She'd been so jubilant, so high on the power of what her determination could produce, that Thad hadn't been able to resist tapping into that excitement.

They had loved for hours on end, and with an energy that surpassed anything he'd ever experienced, as if they'd been transported to another plane of existence, a world where every emotion and every physical pleasure was intensified to the nth degree. But afterward, when Thad had come down from the high, he'd crashed like a junkie without his drug of choice. How could he possibly give her up, if it came to that?

He'd been so damn blithe about raising her grade to a B, but the task had proved more formidable than he'd ever imagined. Lindy was intelligent—she could whip through the most complicated chemistry equations and statistical problems without blinking. But when it came to calculus, it was as if she lacked some crucial connection in her brain.

He shouldn't have raised her hopes so high. If she didn't make the grade, it would crush her, and she would leave him. He knew that. What he didn't know was how to survive without her.

"Did you talk to Professor Baldwin?" he asked as Lindy began chopping onions for the stew.

"Mm-hmm."

"And?"

"I can miss one problem on the final and still get a B." She said the words casually, but a small tremor in her voice gave her away.

One problem. That wasn't much margin for error, and the final exam was tomorrow. "The stew won't be ready for a couple of hours," he said with forced cheerfulness. "So we better crack those books."

She nodded glumly.

It was an evening Thad wouldn't soon forget. He'd never seen Lindy quite so full of anxiety. The more he tried to calm her down, the more agitated she became, forcing him to draw on reserves of patience he hadn't known he possessed.

"Why can't I do this?" she cried in frustration after she'd tried three times to come up with the right answer. She ripped the page out of her notebook and wadded it up with sharp, angry movements.

"You *can* do it," Thad insisted. "You knew this stuff backward and forward last week."

"But now I've got it all mixed up in my head."

"Come on, try it again," he cajoled, shoving a clean sheet of paper in front of her. "Finish this one problem and we'll take a break. I'll give you a hint this time."

She pushed the paper away. "Stop badgering me! I can't do any more. I feel like my head is going to explode."

He sighed and closed the textbook. "All right. It's getting late, anyway. A good night's sleep will probably do more for you than finishing one more problem."

She stared into her lap. "Sorry, Thad, I didn't mean to yell. I know you're just trying to help, but it's so frustrating—"

"I know, honey." He took one of her hands into his and forcibly unclenched her fist. "Go on home. Take a hot bath and get to bed. You'll feel better in the morning."

"Could I stay here?" she asked in a tentative voice. "Just to sleep, I mean. I'm so nervous, I'm afraid I'll have insomnia. If you could just hold me for a little while..."

Sleep with Lindy and not make love to her? This would be a new exercise in self-control. "Of course you can stay," he said as he pulled her out of her chair and drew her into his lap. Her body was stiff, like one giant tension knot.

She pressed her face against his hair. "Have I said thank you lately? I can't believe the hours and hours you've put in trying to drum this stuff into my dense head. It can't be much fun."

"I'm not doing this for fun," he reminded her as he stood with her in his arms. He'd never thought of her as fragile, yet right now she looked as breakable as a crystal goblet. "Come on, let's get some sleep."

* * *

Thad wasn't sure what woke him, unless it was the absence of warmth beside him. Lindy, wearing the top to a pair of his red flannel pajamas, had gone to sleep curled up in the crook of his arm, and now she was gone.

It was still dark outside. He turned on the bedside lamp and read the digital clock—not quite five-thirty.

He got out of bed and stumbled into the living room, wearing only the pajama bottoms that went with Lindy's top. He found her hunched over the card table, scribbling furiously. A pile of discarded papers formed a ring on the carpet around her chair, testifying to the fact that she'd been there awhile.

Even as he watched, she broke her pencil in two and tossed it onto the table, then sighed and put her head in her hands.

"Lindy?"

She jumped a good six inches. "Gawd, don't scare me like that."

"What are you doing?"

"I couldn't sleep. Every time I closed my eyes I saw numbers and dots and squiggly lines. If I could just get this one problem—"

"Let me see what you've done."

But she covered up her work with her hands. "No. When I take the test, you won't be there to give me the answers. I have to do this on my own."

"You have to get some sleep," he reminded her.

"I can't sleep." She sighed deeply. "I'm so damn tense." She picked up a fresh pencil and started to work again.

Thad was more than a little tense himself, and seeing the way her soft, red-flannel top curved over her breasts didn't help any, nor did the sight of her long, bare legs curled around the chair. He sauntered toward her, pondering the wisdom of what he was about to do—but only for a moment.

Reaching from behind her, he slipped the pencil out of her grip.

"Thad—"

"I have a terrific idea for working off some of that tension," he said, speaking in a low voice as he nuzzled her neck.

"Thad..."

He reached around her and began to unbutton her pajama top. "This is for your own good," he said as he slipped a hand beneath the soft fabric and curled it around her small, firm breast. Her heartbeat fluttered against his palm as her nipple hardened under his caress.

She reached up with one hand and touched his face in silent approval. Then she was out of the chair and in his arms. She kissed him as if she would devour him, and he felt it in every fiber of his body. There was nothing gentle about the way her tongue dueled with his, or the way she dug her fingernails into his bare back.

"Do you know how much I hate calculus?" she whispered fiercely as she tugged impatiently at the drawstring of his pajama bottoms.

"No, but I have a feeling I'm going to like finding out— whoa! Lindy!" But now that he'd unleashed her, there was no slowing her down. He found himself stepping out of the pool of red flannel at his feet. Only the fear that his knees would buckle and send him crashing to the carpet kept him from letting her ravish him right there.

He grasped her shoulders and pulled her upright. She opened her mouth, as if she might object to being thwarted in her efforts to please him and satisfy herself, but instead she twined her fingers in his hair and drew him down for another hungry kiss.

He scooped her up and carried her toward the bedroom. She continued to explore his mouth with hers, seemingly oblivious to their change of venue.

Their lovemaking had taken on many different moods in the past—fast and frenzied, slow and seductive, but he'd never seen Lindy quite like this, like a baited lioness. She wouldn't stop kissing him long enough that he could get her undressed. Since she obviously had some sort of pleasant curriculum in mind, he finally gave up the struggle and let her work off her tension any way she saw fit.

Without his hands getting in the way, her clothes came miraculously free of her body and went flying through the air. He was struck anew by the beauty of her form, dimly backlit by the light in the hallway. He could have stared at her like that, just like that, for hours on end. He could have spent the rest of the morning just touching her, reexploring all of the secret places that made her quiver with desire. But Lindy was on a one-track course that did not include leisurely caresses.

He was helpless to change the pace—not that he really wanted to. He sighed in wonder as she climbed astride him, and then she was against him and all around him. She felt agonizingly sweet and tight, and he closed his eyes and let himself simply feel the sweet ecstasy of their joining.

She rode him hard, as if trying to escape demons from hell, and all the time she kept up a fascinating monologue. She cursed her calculus professor and the entire realm of mathematics, and then she cursed Thad for pushing her so hard, and he just smiled through all of it, knowing now from experience that she wouldn't remember a word of it later.

Gradually the rhythm slowed, in reverse order of the way things usually went. He could feel her every muscle softening, losing the tension, until she was as supple as a new blade of grass.

She tensed only once more, looking into his eyes as she did, showing him a depth of emotion that never ceased to amaze him. That unguarded look was more powerful than any caress, tipping him into the sweet abyss of satisfaction.

When it was over she wilted against him and shook with silent sobs. By now he was used to the way her emotions overflowed whenever they made love. So he simply held her, stroking her back and finger-combing her tousled hair, murmuring silly endearments.

He hoped she would sleep now. But after a few minutes she gasped and raised her head to look at Thad, her eyes large and round. "Oh, my God."

"What?"

"I see it now." She snapped her fingers. "That problem. I know how to do it." She was out of bed in a flash, pulling the comforter with her.

By the time Thad had found a robe—more to ward off the chill than from any sense of modesty—Lindy was again hard at work in the living room with the quilt wrapped around her. "Did you ever hear of 'afterglow'?" he asked.

"Hush up, I've almost got it. . . ." In a few short minutes she laid down her pencil. "I did it. See?" She held up her paper for his inspection.

He studied it briefly, then nodded. "That's it."

She hugged him impulsively and covered his face with kisses. "Let's go back to bed. Maybe I can still get a couple of hours' sleep. Oh, Thad, thank you. I really was stressed out, and you cured me."

"Any time." They ambled back to the bedroom, his arm loosely around her waist. "You know, you say the damnedest things when we make love."

"I do?"

"I'll tell you about it some time."

Eleven

Thad paced the hall outside Lindy's classroom. He had taken the morning off so he could drive with her to Nacogdoches for her calculus final. She'd seemed in pretty good spirits a few minutes ago, considering her lack of sleep. He hoped she was equally optimistic after she finished.

An hour into the test, some students were already done and leaving the classroom. Every time the door opened, Thad caught a glimpse of Lindy sitting in the front row, her golden head bent over her work, writing furiously.

Soon she was one of only three students left. At the end of the two hours the door opened one last time, and the three stragglers exited with Lindy bringing up the rear. She gave him a tremulous smile but said nothing as they started down the hall side by side. She clutched a sheaf of papers in one hand—a copy of the final, Thad figured.

She was too pale, and her green eyes seemed unusually large. The faint purple shadows beneath them were testimony to her exhaustion, and Thad felt a surge of guilt for pushing her so hard.

"Are you hungry?" he finally asked when her silence started to get to him. "I'll buy you a hamburger."

"A chili dog," she amended.

"Okay, a chili dog. Are you going to tell me how it went, or leave me in suspense awhile longer?"

Her laughter was strained as they left the building. "I guess my mind was so overloaded I didn't even want to talk about it. It was a hard test."

He pointed to the papers she held. "Is that it?"

"Yeah."

"Can I look at it?"

"No." She dropped it into a trash container as they stepped into the parking lot. "Let's not rehash the exam. I'll just wait till my grades come in the mail."

He would go crazy between now and then. "How well do you think you did?" he asked.

She sighed impatiently. "I left one problem blank—I had no idea how to do it. The others..." She shrugged. "I wasn't sure about a couple of them."

Thad's stomach sank. Her performance on the test didn't sound promising. For the first time, the possibility that she would leave him seemed very real, very close.

He also knew, as they entered a local fast-food emporium, that he wouldn't keep his promise to her. He wouldn't let her go without a fight. In fact, if she insisted on leaving, he'd make the biggest, hairiest scene he'd ever made in his life.

If she refused to marry him, could he convince her to stay in Corrigan for as long as their relationship lasted? Then he could work like hell to make sure it lasted forever. But on second thought, he knew he couldn't settle for a limbo sort of relationship like that. Lindy wouldn't, either. She'd once told him that when it came to the two of them, it had to be all or nothing, and she'd been right.

Lindy practically inhaled her chili dog, amazed that she had an appetite. Thad had tried his best to make her eat breakfast that morning before the test, but she'd almost choked on the scrambled eggs and pancakes. Now she scarfed down the dog, a bag of corn chips and a large lime-ade. Nothing had ever tasted so good.

She was just so relieved. Regardless of the outcome, her ordeal was over. In another week or so, she would receive her grades and the duration of her agreement with Thad would be over, too. What would she do if her grade was a C, and not a B? Suddenly her mind raced with possibilities.

She could relocate again, start fresh somewhere else. She would have to live with the pain of losing Thad for a long time to come, but she'd get over it. Eventually. Maybe.

But she didn't *have* to give him up. She could stay and marry him, anyway. She could find a job somewhere nearby that would give her some measure of satisfaction, whether at the nature center or somewhere else. But she would still have to deal with her failure at school, and the fact that Thad knew she'd failed.

Failure. Dammit, why did she have to keep thinking in those terms? A C didn't mean she'd failed. She had succeeded in bringing her grade up, after all. Just not quite as far as she wanted to.

She rattled the crushed ice in her otherwise empty cup. Did she really need straight A's to get into vet school? Perhaps she could call the school and talk to an adviser, find out how badly a C would hurt her chances.

Maybe she could take the class over again. She grimaced at the prospect. Could she put herself through another sixteen weeks of torture?

She studied Thad, sitting across the table from her. He toyed absently with the straw in his chocolate malt and stared out the window, looking stern and inflexible. But he wasn't like that, not really. Much of his seeming sternness was a blustery front, like hard candy hiding a soft center. He had more love inside him than any one human being should, and she'd been the lucky recipient of more than her fair share.

In some ways she'd made his life miserable. And he kept coming back for more. She would never find that kind of love again; she didn't even want to look.

Yes, for Thad she could endure any torture, even another semester of Professor Baldwin.

Thad caught her gaze then, and his eyebrows arched in surprise. "What?" he asked.

"What what?" she countered.

"You were just smiling like you'd figured out the meaning of life, that's all."

She pressed her fingers to her lips. "I was?"

"You know something I don't?"

"Maybe." What she'd just figured out was that she had a choice. She could control her own future—quite a heady discovery. If it weren't for Thad refusing to let her quit, she never would have known the power of her own will.

She touched his hand. "Come on, let's get out of here. I still have to study for my chemistry and statistics finals."

Exactly one week later, Lindy called Thad at the courthouse. "Can you come over for dinner tonight?" The words were calm, carefully modulated, almost a monotone.

"You got your grades?"

She didn't answer him. "Just be here at seven o'clock, okay?"

"With bells on. But Lindy..." She hung up.

She must have received her grades, Thad concluded. And she must have made the B, or why else would she ask him to dinner? *To tell you goodbye, maybe?*

He stewed about it the rest of the day. By the time he showed up at her place, fifteen minutes early, he was so agitated he tripped and nearly broke his leg trying to get up the garage apartment stairs.

Lindy greeted him with a light kiss and a noncommittal expression. He immediately assessed her appearance, but nothing about her paisley print slacks and fuzzy pink sweater gave him a clue as to her state of mind. Other than the fact that her face was a little flushed—probably due to cooking in a hot kitchen—she looked like she always did. Was that good or bad?

Lord, he was getting paranoid.

She made a big show out of taking his jacket and meticulously smoothing the wrinkles out of it as she hung it on the coat tree.

He couldn't stand the suspense a second longer. "You did get your grades, right?"

She nodded.

"And you made a B in calculus!"

But to that she shook her head. "I don't know. I haven't looked yet. I thought we'd look together," she said as she led the way into the small kitchen.

"*What?* Where are they? Let's look, for crissakes."

"In due time," she said serenely as she opened the oven door to check on whatever was in there. Then she gestured extravagantly toward the refrigerator. "There's a nice bottle of Riesling in there. Why don't you open it and—"

He shut the oven door and whirled her around to face him, bringing her nose to nose with him. "Where... are...your... grades?" he asked, carefully enunciating every word. "I think I've developed an ulcer waiting for them. Our whole future is riding on that envelope—or had you forgotten?"

"I haven't forgotten," she said, smiling even in the face of his obvious irritation. "It's just that—it seems pretty silly to base our whole future on the whims of some pea-brained calculus teacher, don't you think?"

He narrowed his eyes until he was peering out at her through mere slits. "Are you trying to back out of our deal?"

"Would you actually hold me to it if I changed my mind?"

"I would drag you kicking and screaming to the altar."

"Oh, you would not. Anyway, that won't be necessary. I'll come willingly." She held her left hand in front of his face and wiggled her fingers. Green fire flashed before his eyes.

His heart jumped into his throat. "You're wearing the ring."

"I was beginning to think you were blind. I've been waving my hands around like crazy, waiting for you to notice."

"But..." It took a moment or two, but the significance of her gesture finally sank in. He still couldn't believe it. "What about your grades?"

"I'm hoping for that B, of course, but if I didn't get it..." She paused, as if gathering courage. "If I didn't get it, I'll take the damn calculus class over again."

Thad had never heard sweeter words in his life. He touched the soft golden halo of her hair. "You mean it, don't you?"

She nodded. "I can't quit now. I want to be a vet and I'll do it, even if it takes me until I'm a hundred years old. I won't give up on us, either, Thad. I love you, and I'll still love you when I'm the oldest graduate the vet school has ever seen."

He was so moved by her fierce declaration that he couldn't get any of his own words past his throat.

"You do still want me, don't you?"

In answer he pulled her against him and kissed her. He was so full of love for her he could feel it oozing out his pores. He was also exasperated with her for putting him through such agony. "When did you decide all this?" he asked.

"I started thinking about it right after I took the final, but it wasn't until today that I decided for sure. Not until I saw that envelope in the mail and the moment of truth was at hand. That's when I knew I couldn't leave. That's when I knew that for the first time in my life I wanted something bad enough to risk everything for it . . . hey, that's our dinner in there,'' she objected as he reached behind her and turned off the oven.

"Whatever it is, I'm sure it will reheat just fine,'' he said as he took her hand and turned toward the bedroom. "How do you feel about a Christmas wedding?''

* * * * *

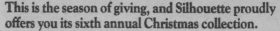

SILHOUETTE®
Desire™

COMING NEXT MONTH

#679 MARRIAGE, DIAMOND STYLE—Mary Lynn Baxter
Fiery-tempered Matthew Diamond took one look at cool
Brittany Fleming and knew she was trouble. But the opportunity to
thaw the big-city ice princess was one he vowed not to miss!

#680 ANGEL FOR HIRE—Justine Davis
Alexandra Logan's prayers were answered when Michael Justice
appeared to help run her refuge for Vietnam veterans. But
what would she do when she discovered he was an absolute
angel—*literally?*

#681 THE STORMRIDERS—Donna Carlisle
Red Worthington and Meg Forrest didn't believe in love at first sight
until they met each other—and married *immediately!* But would love
be enough once the honeymoon was over?

#682 MISS PRIM—Peggy Moreland
When Jack Brannan called in etiquette expert Malinda Compton to
teach his four sons some manners, *he* learned that in his arms,
Miss Prim wasn't so proper after all!

#683 THE LADY AND THE LUMBERJACK—Jackie Merritt
Christy Allen didn't trust men—especially ones like Vince Bonnell.
But when the handsome lumberjack offered the lady logger a helping
hand, Christy found she couldn't let go....

#684 'TWAS THE NIGHT—Lass Small
December's *Man of the Month*, Bob Brown, swore off women after
his divorce. Until he met feisty Josephine Malone and decided she
was one girl he could take home for the holidays.

AVAILABLE NOW:

Angels Everywhere!

Everything's turning up angels at Silhouette. In November, Ann Williams's ANGEL ON MY SHOULDER (IM #408, $3.29) features a heroine who's absolutely heavenly—and we mean that literally! Her name is Cassandra, and once she comes down to earth, her whole picture of life—and love—undergoes a pretty radical change.

Then, in December, it's time for ANGEL FOR HIRE (D #680, $2.79) from Justine Davis. This time it's hero Michael Justice who brings a touch of out-of-this-world magic to the story. Talk about a match made in heaven . . . !

Look for both these spectacular stories wherever you buy books. But look soon—because they're going to be flying off the shelves as if they had wings!

"INDULGE A LITTLE" SWEEPSTAKES

HERE'S HOW THE SWEEPSTAKES WORKS

NO PURCHASE NECESSARY

To enter each drawing, complete the appropriate Official Entry Form or a 3" by 5" index card by hand-printing your name, address and phone number and the trip destination that the entry is being submitted for (i.e., Walt Disney World Vacation Drawing, etc.) and mailing it to: Indulge '91 Subscribers-Only Sweepstakes, P.O. Box 1397, Buffalo, New York 14269-1397.

No responsibility is assumed for lost, late or misdirected mail. Entries must be sent separately with first class postage affixed, and be received by: 9/30/91 for the Walt Disney World Vacation Drawing, 10/31/91 for the Alaskan Cruise Drawing and 11/30/91 for the Hawaiian Vacation Drawing. Sweepstakes is open to residents of the U.S. and Canada, 21 years of age or older as of 11/7/91.

For complete rules, send a self-addressed, stamped (WA residents need not affix return postage) envelope to: Indulge '91 Subscribers-Only Sweepstakes Rules, P.O. Box 4005, Blair, NE 68009.

© 1991 HARLEQUIN ENTERPRISES LTD.   DIR-RL

"INDULGE A LITTLE" SWEEPSTAKES

HERE'S HOW THE SWEEPSTAKES WORKS

NO PURCHASE NECESSARY

To enter each drawing, complete the appropriate Official Entry Form or a 3" by 5" index card by hand-printing your name, address and phone number and the trip destination that the entry is being submitted for (i.e., Walt Disney World Vacation Drawing, etc.) and mailing it to: Indulge '91 Subscribers-Only Sweepstakes, P.O. Box 1397, Buffalo, New York 14269-1397.

No responsibility is assumed for lost, late or misdirected mail. Entries must be sent separately with first class postage affixed, and be received by: 9/30/91 for the Walt Disney World Vacation Drawing, 10/31/91 for the Alaskan Cruise Drawing and 11/30/91 for the Hawaiian Vacation Drawing. Sweepstakes is open to residents of the U.S. and Canada, 21 years of age or older as of 11/7/91.

For complete rules, send a self-addressed, stamped (WA residents need not affix return postage) envelope to: Indulge '91 Subscribers-Only Sweepstakes Rules, P.O. Box 4005, Blair, NE 68009.

© 1991 HARLEQUIN ENTERPRISES LTD.   DIR-RL

INDULGE A LITTLE—WIN A LOT!

Summer of '91 Subscribers-Only Sweepstakes

OFFICIAL ENTRY FORM

This entry must be received by: Nov. 30, 1991
This month's winner will be notified by: Dec. 7, 1991
Trip must be taken between: Jan. 7, 1992—Jan. 7, 1993

YES, I want to win the 3-Island Hawaiian vacation for two. I understand the prize includes round-trip airfare, first-class hotels and pocket money as revealed on the "wallet" scratch-off card.

Name _____

Address_____ Apt. _____

City _____

State/Prov. _____ Zip/Postal Code _____

Daytime phone number _____
(Area Code)

Return entries with invoice in envelope provided. Each book in this shipment has two entry coupons—and the more coupons you enter, the better your chances of winning!

© 1991 HARLEQUIN ENTERPRISES LTD.   3R-CPS